Obsessed

By

Eve Vaughn

This is a work of fiction. Names, characters, places, and incidents are products of the author's imagination or are used fictitiously and are not to be construed as real. Any resemblance to actual events, locales, organizations, or persons living or dead is entirely coincidental.

All trademarks, service marks, registered service marks are the property of their respective owners and are used herein for identification purposes only.

ALL RIGHTS RESERVED
Obsessed
Copyright © 2019 Eve Vaughn
Electronic book publication June 2019

With the exception of quotes used in reviews, this book may not be reproduced or used in whole or in part by any means without permission from the author, Eve Vaughn.

WARNING: The unauthorized reproduction or distribution of this copyrighted work is illegal. No part of this book may be scanned, uploaded or distributed via the Internet or any other means electronic or print, without the author's permission. Criminal copyright infringement without monetary gain is investigated by the FBI and is punishable by up to 5 years in Federal Prison and a fine of $250,000. For more information regarding the government's stance on copyright infringement visit: http://www.fbi.gov/ipr.

Eve Vaughn

Dedication

To my readers, thank you so much for supporting me, and keeping me going. I hope you'll enjoy reading this book as much as I've enjoyed writing it.

And a special thanks to Gwen for always being there for me. Thank you for being a friend. If you threw a party and invited everyone you knew. You would see the biggest gift would be from me and the card attached would say...

Prologue

Copenhagen

"Really, Blaise, if the child wanted to see dancers, couldn't we have at least gone to the Royal Theatre instead of this place with…these people? These street performers." The ferocious frown lines on Lisbeth's face, as she spoke with obvious distaste, ruined the effect of her cool blonde beauty.

It was on the tip of his tongue to tell her she hadn't been invited but Blaise was inclined to be indulgent. Seeing the joy on his young sister's face more than made up for his lover's petulance. "Perhaps, you'd prefer I call my driver to take you home? Aneka and I will stick around a little longer." There was no hidden meaning in his words but Lisbeth seemed to think there was.

She shook her head vehemently. "Oh, no. I wouldn't dream of leaving the two of you here. Not when we are having so much fun. I simply pointed out if dear Aneka wants to see real dancing, you should get tickets to the ballet. Besides, it can't be good for her to be around all these people. She tires so easily and I do so worry about her."

The adolescent in question looked up at the statuesque beauty with a wry grin tilting her lips. "My legs may not work, but my hearing is just fine."

Blaise threw his head back and released a loud chuckle. "That it is, little one."

Red splotches colored Lisbeth's cheeks. "Really, Blaise. You shouldn't encourage her. What she needs is a mother to guide her on how to address her elders and to be more lady-like."

Blaise raised a brow. "I suppose you're volunteering for the job?"

Lisbeth brushed away an imaginary speck of dust off of her immaculate white linen jacket. "You could do a lot worse, and we've been dating for several months now. It's time we move forward with our relationship."

"Is that so?" he asked softly.

"Yes. I think I've been quite patient up to this point, considering you're not the only eligible bachelor in Copenhagen. My family's name is old and respected."

"Ah, I see. While mine is not?" He knew exactly where she was headed. His father had been a salesman of medical equipment. He had eventually started his own business selling directly to medical facilities. His father had worked hard to make his company a success. When Blaise had taken over, he'd turned it into a multi-national conglomerate. They held the lion's share of the European market even though his company sold products all over the world.

Obsessed

He realized some of the 'old money' families looked down their aristocratic noses at his lack of pedigree, though no one would say it to his face. His bank account was large enough to grant him entrance into the upper echelons of society—which he didn't give a damn about. He wasn't ashamed of where he'd come from. His father had worked hard for everything they'd had, as did Blaise. His only regret was his parents were no longer around to enjoy the fruits his labor.

This time. Lisbeth's entire face turned bright red. "You're deliberately misunderstanding me."

"No, my dear. I understand you perfectly."

Aneka's gasp caught his attention. "Oh, Blaise, look!" She pointed in the direction of one of the three stages several meters away. "I think the American dance troupe I read about in the program is about to begin. Can we please go over there?"

Blaise smiled down into his sister's upturned face. "Of course, precious." He wheeled her toward the stage not bothering to check if Lisbeth followed. The angry click of heels behind him told him that she had. Not that it mattered. Today was about Aneka, not his petulant lover who was really making him rethink their relationship.

Maneuvering Aneka's chair down the aisle, he found a couple of empty seats on the end enabling him to sit next to her. Blaise paid little heed to Lisbeth when she took the chair next to him with a dramatic huff. He focused his attention on the stage. Two dancers clad in long-sleeved, flesh-colored unitards moved to the center of the stage, one man, one woman. They moved to a kneeling position with bowed heads. Soft music blared from the speakers as they were joined by two more dancers. The first two stood and they all moved together to the beat of the music. Four more dancers joined them.

Blaise wasn't as enthused about dance as his sister, but the choreography was unlike anything he'd ever seen before. The movements of the dancers were fluid and had the audience including himself riveted. And finally, one last dancer came whirling on stage in a series of spins, moving so fast he could only wonder how she didn't pass out from getting dizzy. And just as quickly, she halted, her back to the audience. Slowly, she gyrated to the music. She moved so sensually Blaise's breath caught in his throat. And then, it happened.

When she turned around, it felt as if someone had punched him square in the stomach because all the breath whooshed out of his lungs. She was magnificent. Unlike the others, her spaghetti strapped unitard was bright red, a contrast to her dark skin. Hugging her body like a second skin, it brought attention to every line of her compact frame. She was obviously the principal dancer.

Though slender, she was a bit curvier than any dancer he'd ever seen, particularly her ass. And what an ass it was. The gentle swell of her breasts was emphasized by an impossibly tiny waist. His large hands would easily circle her midsection.

Gorgeous. Absolutely stunning. Hair pulled back in a tight bun emphasized high cheekbones and a regal facial structure. Her lips were so full they looked to be set in a permanent pout. And, her eyes were huge saucers in her small perfectly sculpted face. He couldn't quite make out their color but her eyes looked dark from where he sat.

She leaped into the air and was caught in the capable arms of one of the male dancers before being tossed to another. Though there was nothing overtly sexual about the choreography, the sensual way in which the tiny dancer moved to the music was damn near erotic. He'd heard the English phrase 'poetry in motion' before but never knew what it had meant until now.

Blaise couldn't tear his gaze away from the stage, even if he had wanted to. Captivated was the only word he could think of, as he watched the American dancers on stage—watched her. He only had eyes for her.

"They're all so good," Aneka's whisper of awe barely registered.

Blaise grunted in response incapable of speech.

And then, the dancers raced off the stage and poured into the aisles, moving around the audience. His body seized up, tightening with awareness. She was only a few meters away and he could make out each feature perfectly, committing them to memory. She was even lovelier up close.

The troupe danced around the crowd and as she moved by, his lady in red as he'd first thought of her, she looked down at Aneka and smiled revealing two devilishly deep dimples. But just as quickly as it appeared, the smile vanished as if he'd only imagined it. He would have killed for that smile.

She returned to the stage alone this time and danced and whirled around in an impressive display of her flexibility. Moments later, she was joined by one of the male dancers. They moved in perfect sync, their bodies grinding against each other so closely; it almost felt as if he was viewing something that should have been behind closed doors. An unfamiliar emotion seared through his body, his chest tightening and hands clenching at his sides, at seeing this man's hands on his lady in red, caressing her as if it were his right.

"Vulgar," Lisbeth snorted with no little disdain.

Blaise lifted his hand to halt any other comments she may have had, yet he never turned his gaze away from the stage. He couldn't, even if he wanted to. Well and truly under the little nymph's spell, his cock jumped to painful attention as he let his imagination roam. It was him on stage, holding and lifting her, running his hands down her body as if they were lovers. He was so caught up in the fantasy, he didn't realize the music had stopped and the routine was over.

Aneka tapped his shoulder. "Wasn't that wonderful, Blaise? I wish I could dance like that."

He barely managed to tear his gaze off the stage before offering his little sister a smile of reassurance. She was staring down at her legs with a rueful expression on her face. "You will dance one day, precious."

Her face lit up. "Do you think I'll be as good as the lady on stage?"

"Of course, you will." Blaise smoothed back a strand of her blonde hair.

"It's really unkind of you to keep giving the child false hope, Blaise." Thankfully, Lisbeth didn't speak loud enough for Aneka to hear but he was more than fed up with her unsolicited opinions.

"That's enough." He pulled out the mobile phone from his breast pocket and dialed his driver. "Brandt, *Frøken* Sorensen requires a ride home. Can you be outside of the festival in ten minutes?" Once he made the arrangements, he replaced the phone into his pocket.

Lisbeth's mouth fell open. "I never said I wanted to leave."

Blaise stared at her through narrowed eyes. "But, I'm telling you to. We'll talk later."

"But Blaise—"

"I said later."

She flared her nostrils and tightened her lips into a thin line. But, there must have been something in his eyes that made her pause for a moment. Lisbeth pasted a smile on her face, leaned over and gave him a kiss on the cheek. "Of course, we'll talk later, darling."

She stood up and scooted by him. She dropped a light kiss on Aneka's cheek. "Goodbye, sweet child."

When Lisbeth's back was turned, Aneka wiped her cheek. Though his sister had never said anything against his lover, Blaise had always gotten the impression that all was not as it appeared between the two of them. Now, he knew. Yes, it was definitely time to re-evaluate his relationship.

"Did you enjoy the show, precious?"

"Oh, yes! It was beautiful. I wish we could meet the dancers."

That sounded like an excellent idea, although there was only one dancer he was interested in meeting. It just so happened, he knew a few of the event organizers. Setting up a meeting with this dance group may not be so difficult. After making a few phone calls, he found himself wheeling Aneka to the back of stages and to a little house where the performers changed. He was met by one of the organizers and led inside.

They were taken to the back of the house where his friend led them to a room full of dancers and well-wishers. Immediately, he sought out his woman in red. She was nowhere to be found. Swallowing his disappointment, he wheeled Aneka inside and was introduced to the troupe by the coordinator. A young man walked over to him who he recognized as one of the dancers—the one who'd danced with his mystery lady. He hated this man on sight but quickly swallowed this irrational emotion as best he could.

"Herr Lundgaard, I'm honored that you've come to our little show." The man held out his hand.

Blaise resisted the urge to ignore it and gave the man's hand a quick shake. "Blaise, please, and you are?"

"Landon Campion, the founder and choreographer of the Bodies in Movement Dance Troupe. We've only been around for a couple years but we've built up a nice fan base."

"And you have a new worshiper—in my sister. She's a big fan of dance."

Landon smiled down at the adolescent. "And, I'm glad you enjoyed it...?"

"Aneka. And yes, it was very lovely."

He shook her hand. "And, it's very lovely to meet you. Let me introduce you to the rest of the dancers."

Blaise appreciated how the young man made sure Aneka met all the dancers in the troupe but he still didn't like him. The way those two danced together, spoke of a familiarity Blaise didn't like one bit. Where was his lady in red? It was as if she'd disappeared off the face of the planet.

They were in the dressing room for a good half hour, all the introductions made when Blaise finally decided to ask for her whereabouts. "Landon, your principal dancer—Aneka was looking forward to meeting her in particular. Is she around?"

"Oh? Kaia? She wasn't feeling well so she's gone back to the hotel."

Disappointment cut through him more than he would have expected it to. "I see. But this festival is supposed to last another few days. Perhaps, we can come by another time."

Landon shook his head with a lopsided grin. "Unfortunately, we'll be heading to London tomorrow and staying there for a few days before going back to New York. We're on a strict schedule."

"Have you any plans to return to Copenhagen?" Blaise felt foolish for pursuing this matter. He'd never been compelled to chase a woman before in his life yet he could think of nothing but meeting her. If he could only see her up close face-to-face, perhaps, this instant pull he felt toward her would fade and he'd be able to breathe again.

Landon shook his head. "We wish. We loved it here but our funding is limited. As a matter of fact, when we go back to the States, I'll be busting my ass trying to find new backers."

Blaise smiled. Maybe, this would be his way in. He reached into his pocket and produced a business card. "Perhaps, you can give me a call and we can discuss your finances should you find you're in need of investors."

The young man's mouth popped open in apparent disbelief. "Are you serious?"

"I'm always quite serious about money." He glanced down at his sister. "Are you ready to go, precious?"

Aneka nodded. "Yes. But Landon, could you please tell your principal dancer she was really good?"

The young man grinned at the girl. "I'll be sure to pass it along."

"Be sure that you do." Blaise nodded his goodbyes before maneuvering Aneka's chair out the room.

He realized then and there he'd do whatever it took to meet the lovely Kaia. The only problem was; he had a feeling she could very well become an unhealthy obsession for him. Little did he realize, she already had.

Obsessed

Chapter One

Kaia's muscles screamed for relief but she continued her stretches to keep her body limber for the grueling routine she was about to perform. Landon had choreographed a new dance sequence which would put her in positions that would make most contortionists cry for mercy. While she was used to his complicated pieces, she had to admit, he'd outdone himself this time. Though Kaia felt no false modesty about her talent, this dance would test her abilities to its limits. She knew how important this night was for Landon, hence the new choreography and his current state of agitation.

Personality wise, Landon was generally easygoing but to work with him was a completely different story. He was a hard taskmaster and required nothing short of perfection, although he was even harder on himself. Not that Kaia could blame him. He'd built Bodies in

Motion from his own blood, sweat, and tears and within a few short years had garnered a name for them. However, if he was tough before, these past weeks he'd been nearly impossible to work with, demanding longer hours and faultless movements. He'd been tense and cranky, barking orders and dishing out criticism for one single misstep.

He was wound so tight, he'd sent Patty, one of the dancers running out of the studio in tears earlier in the week. It took hours for Kaia to convince Patty to return, explaining how their troupe's survival rested on this performance. If Kaia didn't know how important the show tonight was for him, boyfriend or not, she would have given him a piece of her mind.

She'd been there when he'd received the crushing news that one of their corporate backers would be withdrawing their sponsorship by the end of the year. For their small company that not only depended on ticket sales and fundraising to remain in the black, losing a corporate sponsorship would be a terrible setback.

Landon couldn't understand what had happened, considering the head of the endowment fund had been quite fond of their little troupe and was a huge contributor to fine arts programs. For weeks, Landon busted his ass trying to find other backers but in this economy; the task was challenging. Then last month, Landon had come rushing into their loft excited that he had a new potential backer. Apparently, he'd been in contact with some big wig from Europe he'd met while they'd been in Denmark. Landon had been given a business card which he'd lost. However, he had been contacted by the guy's personal assistant who informed Landon that her boss would be in town and was interested in seeing a show. Landon took that to infer that if said bigwig liked what he saw, they'd have a new sponsor, hence the fancy new choreography.

A pair of heavy hands fell on her shoulders and squeezed them lightly. "You good, babe?"

Kaia brought her legs beneath her and used her hands to push herself into a standing position. She turned to face him. Normally Landon was cool as a cucumber before a performance, but he was actually shaking. Kaia placed her hand on the side of his face. "I'm as ready as I'll ever be. The question is, are you good?"

His lips twisted into a half smile-half grimace. "Is it that obvious?"

She brushed an errant curl from his forehead. "A little. You've been pacing backstage as if this is the first time you've performed in front of people."

He released a deep sigh. "Yeah. I don't think I've felt this way since I auditioned for Julliard. Babe, I think you know how important this night is for us. If we don't absolutely knock Blaise Lundgaard's socks off, I'm not really sure how much longer we'll be able to keep the company going."

Kaia nibbled on her bottom lip. "Is it that serious?"

Landon winced. "More than I let on, actually. We lost two more backers."

A gasp escaped Kaia's lips. Landon took care of every aspect of the company, including the business side. Kaia had offered to help him wherever she could and only recently had he relented enough to allow her to choreograph a few pieces here and there. The business aspect, however, he did all on his own. It was no wonder he'd been so stressed lately. "Oh, hon, why didn't you say anything?"

He ran his fingers through his hair with an impatient sigh. "I didn't want you to worry. Besides, it just happened a few days ago. It's like we've become poison or something. We lost some of our sponsors with no warning. One I can understand, two could be a coincidence but the third? Not to mention that endowment I was counting on...." he finished with a sigh.

"We didn't get it?"

He shook his head in response.

"I don't understand. It was as good as yours."

"So, I thought. But the head of the board decided to award it to another fine arts program. I can't seem to catch a break lately."

"How bad are things?"

"Well, we still have a few backers left and I can still pay the dancers and take care of company expenses for another three to four months, five if I make some drastic cuts."

"But this guy in the audience tonight—Lunderberg-Lindbar? What did you say his name was?"

"Blaise Lundgaard. I can't believe you've never heard of him."

Kaia shrugged. "Should I have?"

"I guess not if you don't read the Wall Street Journal or other business magazines. He owns one of the largest medical supply companies in the world. The guy is a billionaire!"

"And, this is the man you met in Copenhagen?"

"Yes, if we're lucky, this guy can be the answer to our problems."

"But, would he be willing to finance the company for the amount you've lost from the sponsors who've backed out?"

"I don't know, but when his personal assistant contacted me, it was like a godsend. Someone must be looking out for us because he's in New York for the next few months and he wanted a ticket to our show, so we're going to make sure we dance like we never have before. Can you do that for me, babe? Give it all you got?"

"I always give one hundred percent."

"I'm going to need 110."

Kaia gave Landon a quick peck on the cheek. "We'll knock the old guy's socks off."

"He's not—" Landon was cut off by the audience's applause signaling the first piece was complete. She was up. She winked at Landon, before rushing to the stage. She nodded her head in acknowledgment to her fellow dancers as they moved past her.

Kaia crouched in a kneeling position. Taking a deep breath, she immersed herself into the scene she was about to dance out. Every performance she gave her all—heart, body, and soul, but tonight she had to give even more. She couldn't let Landon down no matter what.

The music began with a soft crescendo. As the curtains slowly rose, she shot her arms out and began to sway to the beat. She slithered her way to a standing position before bending backward to a bridge. She brought one leg up and then another until she was standing on her hands. Kaia moved her legs into a split before placing her feet on the floor once more. As the music picked up, she pirouetted across the stage, pointing her toes just a little bit harder and stretching out her arms just a little farther.

She contorted her body to the music allowing it to flow through her being, becoming one with it. She was the rhythm. Kaia and the music were one as she grape-vined to a stag jump followed by a calypso leap. By the time the music hit its climax, she was completely lost in its beat. Whenever she jumped, she swore she touched the sky and with each tempo change of the song, she felt a different emotion, expressing it in her movements.

Toward the end of her number, she barely registered that she was joined on stage, but she leaped into her partner's capable hands, trusting him to catch her. Their limbs intertwined and their hands moved over each other's bodies. They moved apart, yet still dancing in sync. By the end of the number, their arms were locked around each other, and tears ran down her cheeks.

Landon brushed them away before the next piece began sending their bodies into another whirl of motion. By the end of the show, Kaia was emotionally drained and her body ached from exertion.

"Babe, you were fantastic!" Landon whirled her around. "I know I said to give it something extra, but you definitely went above and beyond. Did you hear the audience? Two standing O's!"

Kaia chuckled toweling away the sweat from her forehead. "Only two?"

"You did your thing, Kaia!" Patty congratulated her as she approached them.

"Thanks, girl. But, I owe it all to Landon's fantastic choreography."

"I think we should all go out tonight and celebrate. How about we head to Gio's in Little Italy? My treat," Landon announced.

"I'm down!" Patty grinned.

Landon nodded in her direction. "Let everyone else know."

Patty gave Landon a military salute. "Will do, boss." She sauntered off toward the dressing room.

Kaia raised a brow. "Fancy. Are you sure you can handle it?"

Obsessed

"After what you did out there on stage, I got a feeling that we'll soon have the answer to our problems."

"That sure, huh?"

He wrapped his arm around her waist and dropped a light kiss on her lips. "Very sure."

"In that case, I better go back to the loft and get ready for our big night out."

"Don't you want to stick around? Blaise may come backstage and meet the dancers."

"I'm really not up to meeting anyone tonight. I'm too jittery. And if this guy is as good as in the bag as you think he is, then I'm sure we'll eventually meet one day or another."

"Okay, but I'll probably be here for another couple of hours."

"That's fine. I can use that time to decompress and maybe catch a quick nap."

"Do you need money for a cab?"

She shook her head. "I'm good. I planned on walking anyway. It's a nice night."

An uneasy expression crossed his face. "I'm not sure it's a good idea for you to walk home at this time of night."

She waved her hand dismissively. "It's not that late, and our place is only a few blocks away. I'm a big girl. I can take care of myself."

"Okay, just promise to call when you get to the loft or else I'll worry."

"I promise." She gave him a quick peck on the lips and headed to the dressing room to gather her belongings.

Kaia made her way through a throng of dancers complimenting everyone on a great performance and receiving some praise of her own. Normally she stuck around with the rest of the dancers and left the building with everyone else, but tonight she needed some time to herself. She'd never danced like that in her life and it did something to her.

When she made it back to the dressing room, she threw on a pair of jeans and a pullover to cover her leotard. After quickly gathering her things, she left out the back exit.

As she headed home, her body still trembled from her performance. There was no high that could match what she felt now. No drug or aphrodisiac could make her feel so alive. Kaia's mother used to say she came out of the womb dancing. Her mother had taught at a dance studio with dreams of one day opening her own, but when Kaia's father left them for another woman; Cynthia Benson took another job just to make ends meet. But, she had passed on her love of dance to Kaia. One of her mom's proudest moments was seeing Kaia accepted into the top performing arts college in the country before losing her battle to breast cancer.

Kaia wiped away a silent tear as she thought of her mother, wishing she could have seen Kaia perform tonight. She knew her mother would be proud of her for living out her dream as a dancer. The living she made was a modest one. She made just enough to pay her bills. She could have worked for a larger dance company, had even had offers after she'd graduated from Julliard. However, there was something about Bodies in Motion that she couldn't walk away from. Landon Campion was a young up and coming choreographer who had fresh moves and brought new life to movements that had been done thousands of times before. Not to mention, she'd had a bit of a crush on him from their days at school together, though she'd been a first-year student when he was in his forth.

Obsessed

Despite the other offers she'd received after graduation, a chance meeting with Landon had her checking out his newly formed troupe. He'd offered her the role of principal dancer, a position usually reserved for someone with more experience, but he'd believed in her and in turn, she gave her loyalty to him.

Their friendship had soon blossomed into something more. Kaia had never had a boyfriend before Landon, mainly because she'd devoted her life to her craft, but she knew he was the one. She loved him and he loved her. One day when their careers were where they wanted them to be, they would marry, maybe even have a couple kids. But until then, she was content with what they had. He was not only her lover, but he was her best friend.

A smile curved her lips as she practically skipped the rest of the way home. Tonight, there had been magic in their performance. She just knew something exciting was going to happen and the company would be saved.

Blaise considered himself a patient man, but what little he had left was running thin. This was the second time she'd eluded him, and he made a mental note that there wouldn't be a third. For the past three months, he'd thought of nothing but her. At first, he'd tried to forget her, brushing it off as just a passing fancy, but every time he closed his eyes, he dreamed of her—saw her dancing…saw them together.

He thought of how she'd feel in his arms, what she'd taste like. Would she be a quiet lover taking every inch of him in silence as she stared into his eyes? Or would she be a screamer, crying his name until her throat was raw? Either way, he couldn't stop imagining what it would be like to finally have her beneath him. Blaise knew he was crazy for falling so hard for a woman he'd never met before. For all, he knew she could be shallow, or unintelligent, avaricious, or just plain boring. Maybe the fantasy was far greater than the reality, but the obsession would not abate.

Blaise allowed a few weeks to pass, waiting for his thoughts of her to fade to a distant memory. He'd thrown himself into his work, and spending time with his sister, but when those two things failed to distract him, he realized he'd need—no, *have* to pursue this or else he'd literally drive himself insane.

His first step was to hire someone to dig up all the information they could on the little American dance company known as Bodies in Motion and its principal dancer.

Kaia Benson...

He liked the sound of her name. Blaise practiced saying it over and over again. He loved the way it rolled off his tongue. Twenty-three years old. Graduated from Julliard. Lived in New York with her boyfriend who was also the founder of Bodies in Motion. That last piece of information had Blaise gnashing his teeth together. Mother was deceased. Father lived in the Philadelphia suburb of Doylestown with his second wife and two children, a son and daughter. From what the investigator had dug up, Kaia didn't have much of a relationship with her surviving parent. She danced mainly with Bodies in Motion but also volunteered her time at a youth center in Harlem giving underprivileged children dance lessons. The report contained other minute details, but these were things he wanted to learn from her. And, he intended to do just that.

As for the second part of the investigation, he learned that Bodies in Motion didn't do too badly bringing in revenue as far as ticket sales and merchandise, however, they still relied heavily on corporate sponsorship and private donations.

That is when he set his plan in motion. He had his man find out about every single sponsor and whether his L Corp, the conglomerate he headed, was connected with said businesses in any way and then he played the waiting game. Waiting for Campion to contact him as Blaise was sure he would when the dance company's backers "suddenly" withdrew sponsorship.

In the meantime, he made plans to take up temporary residence in New York. A year ago, he'd learned of only three doctors in the world who performed a new stem cell procedure to heal and regenerate healthy cells in damaged nerves, thus restoring mobility to paralyzed body parts. One was in Japan, the other in Switzerland and the last in New York. Blaise had done the research and it was just his luck that the originator of said surgery was the doctor in New York. And being that he'd settle for nothing but the best, he knew New York was where he'd take his sister to get her surgery. He'd already intended to take Aneka there once she finished her studies for the semester.

Knowing Kaia was in New York just made it seem that fate had brought her to him. That she was meant to be his and his alone.

By the time he and his sister had settled in their temporary new home in Manhattan, he still hadn't heard from Campion although he'd been assured that his plan had taken effect. Impatient to get what he wanted, he had his assistant reach out to the man he now considered his rival.

And now his plan was almost at its fruition. After directing his assistant to connect with Campion, Blaise was met with the other man's surprised delight. Campion had said he'd lost the business card he'd been provided or else he'd have been in contact sooner and that he was anxious to discuss sponsorship. He'd played right into Blaise's hands.

Campion had invited him to a show and Blaise, not wanting to miss a chance to see his tiny dancer again, accepted. Yet here he was again, in a familiar scene, backstage after a performance with the lovely Kaia nowhere to be found. Blaise had been glad he'd left Aneka home with her companion because the entire time Kaia had been on stage, his dick was rock hard. It was as if she had danced just for him. If he'd thought her moves sensual the first time he'd set eyes on her, they were downright erotic this time around. He hadn't been able to tear his gaze away from the stage even if he wanted to. She was even more beautiful than he remembered and he was just as determined to have her.

At the end of the show, he could barely wait to get backstage and finally see her—touch her.

"Blaise?"

Blaise was brought back to reality at the sight of the slight frown on Campion's face. Forcing a smile to his lips, he focused his attention on the other man. "My apologies, what were you saying?"

Campion released an uneasy chuckle. "You seem a bit distracted. I was asking if everything is okay."

"Everything is fine. So, your principal dancer...Kaia, did you say her name was? Will she be returning anytime soon?"

"No, she's taken off for the night. But a bunch of us will be meeting for dinner later on in Little Italy. She'll be there. You're welcome to come."

Blaise reached down deep to hide the distaste he felt. The last thing he wanted to do was to share Kaia with a bunch of people in a crowded restaurant. He shook his head with mock regret. "I must decline, unfortunately. I need to get home and check on my sister. She's still settling in. Speaking of Aneka, I know she would enjoy meeting you all again, particularly Kaia as we didn't have the privilege the last time we saw her dance. Perhaps, you and your dancers would like to join me at my penthouse for a private get together...say tomorrow night? And afterward, we can discuss finances." He knew it was short notice but frankly, he didn't give a damn. Blaise refused to wait another full day without seeing her, particularly when she was within his grasp.

"Of course. That would be great. We'll all be there."

"Just make sure that you all are. If I'm to invest in your company, I'd like to see the entire product."

Campion nodded enthusiastically. "Of course. Does this mean...?"

Blaise nodded. "After that performance how could I not, as I said, we'll go into further detail tomorrow. I'll have my assistant call you in the morning with my address and what time you need to show up. You can pass it on to the rest of your troupe."

"Of course." Campion shook his hand profusely. "Thank you so much. I look forward to working with you."

When Campion released his hand, Blaise turned his back barely able to hide his smirk. Everything was going according to plan.

Chapter Two

Blaise did his best to play the gracious host, greeting his guests and making sure they were comfortable in his home. But as each new arrival joined the party and it wasn't who he'd been expecting, his disappointment and impatience grew. Where the hell was Campion or Kaia? They should have been here over a half hour ago.

He took another swig of his scotch to chase away his building annoyance. Currently, he was in the middle of a conversation with someone named Patty or Penny. He didn't hear a word she said. He simply nodded at the appropriate intervals giving the appearance of an interest he didn't have.

Blaise glanced across the room to where his sister held court. Three dancers surrounded her and Aneka wore one of the largest smiles he'd seen her sport in a while. At least, she was enjoying herself and for that, he was grateful. Had she not exhausted herself shopping with her companion the day before, he would have taken her to the performance with him. But, it was just as well. By the end of the night, he'd practically own Campion's little dance company and his sister would be able to see as many performances as she wanted. Maybe Blaise would even request private performances just for her.

From the look of delight on her face as she interacted with the dancers, he could tell she was in heaven. Making his sister smile was one of his missions in life, considering how much she'd already been through in her twelve years. Having lost their parents in the same car accident that left her paralyzed from the waist down, she'd experienced a series of operations and missed out on many experiences girls her age had. Yet, she never complained. Instead, she endured with a courage that left Blaise in awe. He hoped one day she'd get the use of her legs back so she'd be able to fulfill her potential to its limits.

"Mr. Lundgaard?"

The redhead's nasal voice broke through the barrier of his thoughts. Blaise focused his attention on her.

"My apologies, Polly. What were you saying?"

A hint of red stained her cheeks as if she were embarrassed. "It's Patty, actually."

He grinned ruefully, "Again, I must offer my apologies. I am terrible with names, so please don't take it personally. I don't know how I could have forgotten the name of a woman as lovely as you." He took her hand and brought it to his lips, his gaze locking with hers. He was actually quite sharp when it came to remembering names—or at least the ones he cared to remember, but there was no point in needlessly humiliating the poor woman.

Obsessed

This time Patty's face turned bright red, as she let out a peal of high pitched giggles. "Are you flirting with me, Mr. Lundgaard?"

He smirked. "Depends. Do you like it?"

She giggled again. "You're putting me on, of course."

"I never tease, especially beautiful women. And it's Blaise." He was laying it on thick, but he sensed that Patty was the type with loose lips. If he buttered her up, he could perhaps find out a few things from her.

She flipped a lock of long red hair over her shoulder and wiggled her eyebrows. "If you keep it up, you might give a girl ideas."

He brought the glass of scotch to his lips while still maintaining eye contact. "And we wouldn't want that, would we?" It was time to pull back. Blaise only needed her to be flattered a little, not to the point where she misread any signals. "Tell me," he quickly changed the subject. "How do you like dancing for Bodies in Motion?"

Patty paused for a moment to furrow her brow as if sensing his withdrawal, but she quickly schooled her features to hide whatever she must have been thinking. "I like it, actually. I never thought I'd end up dancing for such a small dance company. After all, I've danced in multi-million dollar productions in Vegas."

Blaise raised a brow. "You were a showgirl?"

Patty scrunched up her nose in apparent distaste. "No. I danced with some of the top choreographers in the world."

"I see." Blaise didn't really, but he wanted her to keep talking. "So how did you end up with Bodies in Motion?"

"After my last contract in Vegas was up, I wanted a change of scenery. The competition is something fierce over here and I wanted to prove to myself that I could make it in the big apple. I happened to hear about an up and coming troupe and I've got to admit, I was impressed. Landon's choreography is like nothing I've seen in a long time and I've been dancing since I was two. The money may not be the best, but to dance under such brilliance was a challenge I couldn't pass up."

"Brilliant, eh? You think Campion is going places?"

"Most definitely. Usually, I would stay away from startups, but Landon...I don't know. There's something about him. It's like he's the second coming of Fosse, Astaire, and Taylor combined. You only have to see him in action to know it. He's not only a fantastic choreographer but a brilliant dancer. It's an honor to work with him."

"And, what is it like working with the company's principal dancer? I'm not much of an expert on dance myself, but from what I can tell, she's no slouch."

"Oh, Kaia? She's...as far as ability, she's like a female version of Landon...but different."

"How so?" Now that Patty was on to the subject Blaise was most interested in, he paid extra special attention to what she had to say.

"It's different in that, Landon is brilliant, but even with said brilliance, he still has to work hard to maintain that greatness. He puts in a lot of hours at the studio as we all do, but Kaia is almost like a freak of nature. Her talent just seems to come naturally to her. Not saying she doesn't work really hard at what she does, but when she moves, it's hard to concentrate on what you're doing. It's not common for one so young without extensive experience to be a principal dancer in a troupe of any size, but she truly deserves it. One time when I watched her dance, I shed tears."

Obsessed

Blaise could believe it. Watching Kaia dance had made him experience a plethora of emotions, lust being one of them. It gave him pause. Would he still feel the same about her face to face when her body wasn't in constant motion? Would the obsession wane? No, there was something more. There had to be or this was all for nothing. Firmly pushing the thought from his mind, he continued to grill the hapless Patty. "I would imagine with her talent, there must be some jealousy among the other dancers?"

Patty waved her hand dismissively. "That would be in any dance company or in any situation with a group of high achievers. Yes, there is some tension now and then, but not really with Kaia. She's good without rubbing it in people's faces. I think it just comes so natural to her, she doesn't even realize how good she actually is. Honestly, I'd hate her if she weren't such a nice person."

"Nice?" Blaise was intrigued.

"She's a sweetheart. Always willing to help out where it's needed. Landon is a nice guy himself, but truthfully, he can be difficult to work with at times. I truly believe if Kaia weren't there to calm him down, he'd be an absolute nightmare. She's kind of like the peacemaker among us. Whenever some of us are arguing, she's usually the one who resolves the issues. She's the one people go to if they want something from Landon because he rarely denies her anything."

Interesting. The more Patty talked, the more enamored he became of Kaia. The women who he'd associated within the last several years, like Lisbeth for instance, thought of no one else but themselves. Kaia Benson almost sounded too good to be true.

Even though he already knew the answer, he felt compelled to ask, "So Landon and Kaia...they are together?"

Patty nodded. "They are, although there are a couple dancers in the company who wouldn't mind taking Kaia's place if you know what I mean."

"Yourself included?"

"No. Landon's a cutie, but a little too intense for me. Besides, he doesn't have eyes for anyone other than Kaia."

That piece of information didn't sit well with Blaise. In a way, he had hoped Campion wasn't that serious about Kaia, that way Blaise wouldn't feel too terribly when he finally made Kaia his. But upon hearing the other man cared deeply for the object of Blaise's desire, he realized his task wouldn't be accomplished without someone getting hurt. Part of him said to leave it alone, but the other half wouldn't let go of the erotic dreams of her that had him waking in a cold sweat every night since he'd first set eyes on her. He's come this far, and he had every intention of seeing it through. How could he be wrong when he felt like this?

From the corner of his eye, he saw his housekeeper opening the door for two new arrivals. Blaise stilled. Patty forgotten. Entering his penthouse behind Campion was Kaia. He couldn't move, speak or breathe. She looked like the personification of a Nubian goddess. She wore a light orange, spaghetti strap dress that skimmed her figure to perfection and fell a few inches above her knees. Her hair was in a crown of big curls and her dark skin glowed, looking to barely be touched by makeup. She was breathtaking.

Slowly coming out of his temporary paralysis, he walked toward them, vaguely remembering to excuse himself to Patty. As he approached, there were a couple things Blaise noticed; Kaia's hand was clasped firmly in Campion's and she gazed at him with adoring eyes. And, there was something more—a secretive look they shot at each other, the look of two lovers who had been up to something naughty. It was probably why they'd been late to the party and it pissed Blaise off to no end. More than anything, he wanted to crush Campion beneath his heel for daring to touch his woman.

It was too early to show his hand, however. He'd allow the other man to get comfortable around him, and once his guard was finally down, then bam! This wasn't personal on Blaise's end, had Kaia been with anyone else, Blaise would have been equally relentless. In his mind, Campion would be getting the funding his dance company needed, and in return, Blaise would get what belonged to him. Kaia.

He should have felt like an absolute bastard for what he intended to do, after all, it seemed as if Kaia was quite taken with Campion. She probably even considered herself in love with him, but every gut feeling in his being told Blaise that this woman was meant for him. And, only him. What she had with Campion was calf love. She'd get over it.

Kaia fluffed her hair self-consciously, hoping it didn't appear as messy as it had been before she and Landon had left their loft. A slight smile curved her lips as she thought back to why they were late. She'd taken extra care with her appearance tonight because she knew how important this dinner was to her boyfriend. Kaia was a tomboy at heart and preferred her jeans, sneakers, and hoodies when she wasn't dancing. Prettying herself up and being girly was something she had to work at, so when she'd asked Landon to zip her up, he started kissing the back of her neck.

"Landon, stop. We're going to be late if you keep fooling around like this."

He pushed her hair to the side and brushed his lips against the nape of her neck. "You know it drives me crazy when you wear your hair like this and you look…"

"Like a girl?" she teased.

"Babe, you always look like a girl, but you know what I mean. It's always a treat to see you dressed up like this. And this perfume, it's driving me crazy."

A smiled curved her lips. It had been her mother's favorite scent, a concoction she mixed herself using essential oils. Kaia had added her own spin to it, but it was basically still her mother's recipe. She only wore it for special occasions, like tonight. "Well, there's nothing you can do about it now. We can't be late. This party is important to you."

"It is, but I was told it was an informal get-together. Besides, I have it on good authority that this deal is in the bag. The party can wait but the two of us haven't had any real quality time together in some weeks."

She wiggled against him, feeling that all familiar stirring between her thighs. Kaia hadn't seen the romantic, spontaneous side of Landon in days so this was a welcome change, but she felt she needed to offer one more token protest. "But, we should probably get going."

"Says who?" The next thing she knew, his arms were wrapped around her waist and she was pulled into his embrace. As he began to nibble on her ear and move his hands along her ribcage until he cupped her breasts, she melted against him. Damn, she was weak.

Honestly, their relationship had been strained for weeks due to Landon's short temper and hyper-focus on the dance troupe. But now that Kaia was aware of the stress he'd been going through, it was understandable. She was happy to have her boyfriend back.

After a not so quick romp, they'd glanced at the clock to discover they only had fifteen minutes to get dressed and get to the party. Following a quick shower and getting dressed in a hurry, Kaia had ruefully glanced in the mirror to see she didn't look as nice as she did the first time around, but at least she was presentable. Besides, she was sure Mr. Lundgaard would barely spare her a second glance.

Landon squeezed her hand, bringing Kaia back to the present, "Kaia, I'd like to introduce you to Blaise Lundgaard."

Kaia hadn't realized her host had approached them. She lifted her head to see him and found herself craning her neck to meet his gaze. When their eyes connected, an involuntary gasp escaped her lips. She wasn't sure what she'd been expecting, but it hadn't been someone this young. When she thought billionaire, she thought of some stodgy octogenarian, not one this young, or...this good looking. The man couldn't be more than thirty-five or six.

She dropped her gaze, instantly squirming under his intense blue scrutiny. There was something about the way he looked at her that left her slightly uneasy. No one had ever looked at her like that before and she couldn't figure out why. Did she look an even bigger mess than she thought? Again, her hand went self-consciously to her hair.

"It's nice to meet you, Mr. Lundgaard," she murmured, unable to look him in the eyes. She couldn't exactly figure out why, but the man made her nervous. She chided herself silently. He was a human being just like her. There was no reason to feel like this around him. She held out her hand politely to shake his.

"Kaia, it's a pleasure to finally meet you. And please, I'd be insulted if you called me anything other than Blaise." His voice was deep and almost hypnotic in its cadence. She knew he was Danish, but his accent was very faint, it almost had a British lilt to it. He caught the offered hand and held on to it. When he didn't let go of her hand immediately, she raised her gaze to meet his again.

She tried to smile but his stare held her hostage. "Umm, okay."

"Say my name, Kaia," he commanded softly still holding on to her hand.

Kaia moistened her lips with the tip of her tongue. She glanced over at Landon for guidance, yet her boyfriend only nodded with encouragement. Maybe this guy was just eccentric. Either way, she couldn't risk offending him, considering his support for Bodies in Motion hung in the balance. She turned to him again nodded. "Blaise."

His smile held more than a little mischief. "Good. Hopefully, I'll hear you say more of it soon enough." He released her hand but not before giving it one last squeeze. Blaise turned his attention to Landon. "It's good that you could make it. I was beginning to think you weren't interested in my sponsorship."

Landon turned bright red and started to stutter. "I- I'm uh, we—"

Blaise held up his hand with a chuckle. "No need to explain. If I had a beautiful woman like Kaia, I can only imagine the many times I'd be delayed."

At that comment, Kaia could barely hold back a gasp. She didn't know many rich people, but she was pretty sure none of them spoke so freely. She had to excuse herself. "Um, I see a couple people over there I'd like to speak with." Without waiting to hear Landon's response to Blaise's outrageous comments, she hurried over to a few of her friends that were already in attendance.

She just made it across the room when she slammed her knee against something hard and metal. "Ouch!" she exclaimed reaching for her injured joint.

"Oh! I'm so sorry!" A voice below her exclaimed.

Kaia looked down to see a girl in a wheelchair. She looked to be somewhere between 10 and 13. The ache in her knee slowly receded, indicating there was no serious harm. "It's okay. I should be the one apologizing. I wasn't looking where I was going."

The girl offered her a big smile. "That's fine, I'm used to it. My name is Aneka, I saw you dance when your troupe was in Copenhagen and I loved it. I had to meet you."

Kaia stooped down to Aneka's level, not wanting to look down on the kid. "I'm Kaia, nice to meet you, Aneka and thank you. I'm glad you enjoyed it."

Though Aneka's English was excellent, her accent was much more pronounced than Blaise's. The blonde hair and some of the facial features told her that Aneka was some relation to Blaise. Kaia briefly wondered if the girl was his daughter. "My brother was supposed to take me to see the performance yesterday, but I was so exhausted from being out most of the day, he sent me straight to bed. He said I'd see other shows while we're in New York."

Her brother. Kaia wondered where their parents were since Blaise was in charge of his sister. "And, how long will you be in New York?"

"For some months, at least. I have a consultation with the orthopedic surgeon next week about my legs and we'll take it from there. If the doctor gives us the go ahead, I should have surgery next month and afterward, rehabilitation."

Kaia raised a brow. "So, you'll be able to walk?"

Aneka smiled and rubbed her thigh. "Yes. This won't be my first surgery. There have been others, but none have worked. But, Blaise seems to think this one will. It involves stem cells, he said. Do you think it will work?"

Kaia was no expert, but she certainly wasn't going to rain on Aneka's parade. "It sounds like your brother wouldn't have brought you over here if he didn't think it would. Nothing is beyond the realm of possibility."

Aneka let out a sigh of relief. "Good. Lisbeth says I'm getting my hopes up, but what does she know? One day, I will walk and dance."

The dreamy expression in Aneka's eyes when she mentioned dance, tugged at Kaia's heartstrings. Whoever this Lisbeth person was, she sounded like a complete bitch to tell a child something like that. Everyone deserved to have a dream. She didn't know what she'd do if she didn't have the ability to dance, and even though she'd only known this girl for a few minutes, she desperately hoped the surgery was a success. Kaia found herself reaching for Aneka's hand. "You will walk and you will dance."

Aneka's smile lit the room. "As well as you?"

Kaia grinned. "Even better than me."

"Thank you for saying so. I must admit," she lowered her voice and dipped her head, closer to Kaia's, "I'm a little scared, but I won't tell Blaise because he might change his mind about me having the surgery."

"Sweetheart, you don't have to go through with it if you don't want to."

"But, I do. It's just that...I'm so scared of being alone. My companion has had a family emergency and will return home next week."

"I'm sure your brother will be there for you."

"Yes, but he hovers over me. I love him, but he's so overprotective. I wish I had someone else there with me..." Aneka's face brightened as if a light bulb came on. "What about you?"

"Me?"

"Yes. I think the two of us can be great friends."

"I...I don't know. I'm in the dance studio seventy percent of the day and when I'm not, I have other obligations to attend to."

"Oh." Aneka's smile faltered slightly, but not completely.

Kaia felt like such a heel. But she hardly knew this girl, and if she spent time with her that would mean her brother would be around from time to time as well.

"It's okay. I understand."

It was that understanding and the underlying disappointment in Aneka's voice that got to her. "Look, Aneka, like I said, I'm extremely busy, but...I'll see what I can do."

Aneka's smile widened. "Really? I can't wait to tell Blaise!"

"Tell me what, precious?"

"Kaia said she'd be there for me at my surgery!"

Kaia stood up, her mouth hanging open. She hadn't said anything of the sort, but now that she'd given the impression she was stuck.

Blaise stared at her with that ever-intense gaze of his, making Kaia take a step back. "Did you now?"

"I-uh, well, not exactly. I said I'd see what I could do. I mean with my schedule and all—"

"We'll find a way around it," he cut in.

"But, I have obligations."

"I'll handle them." Without warning, Blaise took Kaia by the arm. "Excuse me, Aneka, I need to speak with Kaia privately for a moment. Why don't you go mingle with some of the other dancers?"

"Okay, but Kaia, come back and see me, I wanted to talk to you some more."

Kaia could only nod before she was maneuvered away by Blaise. She looked around for Landon, but he seemed to be engrossed in conversation with two other dancers. She wanted to pull away from Blaise's grasp, but he held her firm.

She found herself on the balcony with him. Once they were alone, he released his grip on her and she immediately backed away putting several feet of distance between them. "Look, Mr. Lundg—"

"Call me that and I will do something that will make you never forget my name again," he threatened taking a step closer.

She stepped backward until she felt the rail of the balcony behind her. "Don't." She held up her hands to keep him away.

"Do I make you uncomfortable?"

Kaia shivered, even though it was warm out. She wrapped her arms around her body. "A little." She didn't want to offend the guy completely, especially if she was being paranoid for no reason.

Obsessed

"I just wanted to thank you is all. I didn't want my sister to hear what I had to say. I couldn't help but notice how at ease you were with her. Most people pretend her disability doesn't bother them, but you can always see it in their faces. My sister is very sensitive to that. She picks up on it quite easily. I haven't seen her so quickly at ease with anyone in a long time. I'd hired a companion for her while we're here in the States, but unfortunately, I found that the companion was more interested in our lifestyle than spending time with Aneka."

"But Aneka said—"

"She said, what I led her to believe. The last thing I want is for my sister to be hurt. But as I was saying, I know how busy your schedule is, but I would like to ask if you would visit her from time to time. Perhaps, I could work something out with your boyfriend?"

Kaia wanted to say no, but she remembered that look on Aneka's face and the word cleaved to the roof of her mouth.

"I..."

"Say yes, Kaia."

Kaia felt as if she was being backed into a corner. "I'm not sure how much time I'd be able to devote to your sister."

"Just a few hours a week is all I ask. I'll make it worth your while."

She shook her head. "I don't want your money."

"Then do it because my sister needs a friend."

"But, she barely knows me. Neither do you. Why would you want some complete stranger around your sister?"

Again, that unreadable expression entered his eyes. "You'd be surprised what I know about you. Look Kaia, I didn't get to where I am by taking no for an answer.

As I will be conducting business with your boyfriend, you'll probably be seeing quite a bit of me. And one thing you'll find out is that I get what I want."

For a second, it didn't seem as if they were talking about his sister. Blaise moved closer. Kaia's eyes widened. She flinched away when it looked as if he'd touch her.

"Kaia!" Landon came out on the balcony. "There you are babe, I was looking for you."

Gratefully, Kaia brushed past Blaise and hurried to Landon's side. She linked her arms through his and held him tight. "Mr. Lundgaard," she emphasized the name, "and I were just talking about his sister. We hit it off and he was asking if I could come visit her from time to time."

Landon raised a brow, looking to Blaise and then at Kaia before an easy smile settled on his lips. "That would be really sweet of you, babe. I think it's a great idea."

Kaia was hoping he'd give her a way out but she realized he probably didn't want to upset the one man who could save Bodies in Motion.

Blaise smirked. "I'll leave you two lovebirds out here for a spell and mingle with the rest of my guests. You won't have many more nights like this...I mean with the weather change occurring soon.

Blaise left them alone then, not looking back.

Kaia, immediately, wrapped her arms around Landon's waist and placed her head against his chest. "Hold me, Landon."

"What's the matter, babe?" He kissed the top of her head.

Somehow, that man had gotten under Kaia's skin and she wasn't sure if she liked it very much. One thing was certain; she intended to stay as far away from him as she could. "I...I don't know. I just don't know."

Chapter Three

"And one and two and three and four. Step, ball change and kick and turn and chest pop!" Kaia demonstrated before watching the class repeat her motions. "Great job, guys. You're all doing terrific. Unfortunately, that's all the time we have for today."

She was met with a roomful of groans. "Ah man, Kaia. Can't we stay just a little longer?" Deena, one of the little girls who took her dance class asked.

"'Fraid not sweetie. We have to clear out for the next class. It wouldn't be fair for the ones waiting if we cut into their time."

"But hardly anyone takes tap," Tanisha, another student argued.

"Even if there were only two people taking tap class, they deserve their turn as well. How would you feel if you were scheduled for a class but had to wait past the time you're supposed to start because the class before you let out late?"

Obsessed

Tanisha let out an exaggerated sigh. "I guess I wouldn't like it that much. But, the hour goes by so fast. You're the best teacher we've ever had."

Kaia's heart warmed at the compliment. "And believe me, it's a pleasure to teach you all. But look on the bright side, I'll be here twice next week." Kaia gently pushed a stray curl off the child's forehead. "Okay class, I'm really pleased with everyone's progress. When we see each other again, we're going to put all the moves we learned together and have a good time. See you later kids and be safe getting home."

The children took their time gathering their belongings. Some of them gave Kaia a hug goodbye, others waved shyly as they headed out. Teaching hip-hop at the youth center in Brooklyn was definitely one of the highlights of her week. She loved children and any opportunity to bring the art of dance to anyone who might otherwise not be exposed to it was always a plus.

Kaia had started teaching for a community service project in college but found that she liked it so much that she continued doing it after her mandatory service was complete.

Kaia grabbed her gym bag and went to the bathroom to change. Once she was done, she glanced at her watch. She was supposed to meet Landon for dinner at their favorite pizzeria and thankfully she had plenty of time to swing by their loft for a quick shower and change as long as she could catch the very next train. Rushing out the door, she didn't notice the sleek luxury vehicle parked in front of the community center until the rear driver's side window slid down and someone called out her name.

"Kaia."

She stiffened. Kaia didn't have to turn around to see who the voice belonged to. The man had made such an impression on her the first time they met, she doubted his voice was one she'd soon forget. She'd gone over her conversation with Blaise Lundgaard a thousand times and wondered if she might have misconstrued what he'd said. His words had not been explicit, but the implication was there all the same. Still, he'd made no effort to contact her in the past week. She knew he talked to Landon a few times about business but nothing else.

She had begun to think that maybe everything was all in her head. So, why the heck was he here in a part of Brooklyn someone like him wouldn't normally be caught dead in? Kaia wanted to keep walking but she couldn't, knowing he was the sole reason Bodies in Motion was still in existence. At the very least, she had to be cordial to the man.

Forcing her lips into a smile, she walked over to the town car and looked inside. Just as she expected, Blaise Lundgaard, lounged in the back looking as if he didn't have a care in the world. "Mr. Lundgaard, what brings you to this part of the city?" she asked as politely as she was able to muster.

He raised a brow as a smirk tilted his well-formed lips. "I figured you to be a smart woman, Kaia. Need you ask when we both already know the answer?"

She took a deep breath and internally counted to ten before answering. "I appreciate your faith in my intelligence, however, I really have a train to catch, Mr. Lundgaard, so I need to go. It was nice seeing you again," she forced the lie out.

His smirk remained. "There's no need to take the train when I have a car at your disposal. Get in. I'll take you wherever you want to go."

She backed away from the car. "That's okay. I don't mind taking the train. I wouldn't want to take you out of the way or waste your time. I'm sure you're a busy man."

"I don't waste time. I wouldn't be here if I didn't want to be. Now please, get in the car, otherwise, I might start to think that you don't like me. It's a shame, considering I would like nothing more than to be on good terms with the dancers for the company in which I finance."

Kaia took another step back when she heard the emphasis on those last words. While he wasn't outright threatening her, the underlying steel in his voice left no room to interpret his statement any other way. She moistened her now dry lips with the tip of her tongue, wishing she would have walked away when she'd heard him call. She could have pretended not to hear. But, it was too late now.

Before she could reply, the rear driver's side door opened, and Blaise stepped out of the car, his height imposing. With a smile, he gestured toward the car. "Please, get in."

By refusing, she could very well cause trouble for Landon, but if she got in, she could cause problems for herself. Blaise Lundgaard made her extremely nervous and she didn't like being out of her element. He reached out and gently cupped her elbow, galvanizing Kaia into action. She snatched her arm away but quickly realized how offensive that may have come off. "Uh, sorry. Um, thanks for the ride." It was just a ride, right? She slid into the back seat, wishing she was anywhere else but here.

Blaise followed behind, closed the door and nodded to the driver to go before she could change her mind. When the car set in motion, he pressed a button on the console which sent the partition up separating them from the driver.

Kaia looked out the tinted window, concentrating on absolutely nothing at all. "I'm going back to my apartment. It's—"

"I know where you live, Kaia." Again, his words though innocent were loaded with innuendo.

She decided not to rise to the bait by asking him how he knew where she lived or where she'd be today. Kaia kept her lips clamped shut.

"I find it admirable that you devote some of your time to disadvantaged children."

"Thanks," she mumbled, still not looking away from the window.

"From the little, I know of you, I think you're a woman of your word, am I correct?"

She squirmed in her seat, unsure of which direction this conversation was headed. "I try."

"So, I trust you'll be in contact with Aneka soon. She's been talking about you nonstop. And, her appointment is coming up. She very much would love for you to accompany her. You haven't forgotten, have you?"

Kaia balled her fists in her lap. "No, I haven't. I intend to contact her soon to make arrangements for a visit. But, I didn't promise I'd be able to go to doctor visits with her. My schedule is pretty hectic with the troupe rehearsing for our upcoming show."

"Ah, yes...the show. And nothing is more important than that, correct?"

"It's important to Landon so therefore it's important to me. Like I said, Mr. Lundgaard, I will be in touch with Aneka. As a matter of fact, I'll give her a call tomorrow. Perhaps, you can arrange something with Landon so she can come by and see a rehearsal.

Landon usually doesn't allow visitors when we're practicing, but I'm sure he'll make an exception for you."

There was a long pause when she finished, but Kaia refused to turn away from the window to gauge what the man beside her was thinking. It was bad enough that she was in such close proximity to him.

"Kaia, do I make you nervous?" he asked silkily.

"I don't know what you're talking about," she bit out through clenched teeth, willing this nightmarish car ride to be over soon.

"Of course, you do, *kæreste*." His words were almost like a soft caress. She didn't need to understand Danish to know he'd whispered some type of endearment. "I have a question for you. Do you love Campion?"

Kaia stiffened. What the heck did that have to do with anything? "With all due respect, I don't think it's any of your business but yes, I do."

"Do you love him enough to do anything for him?"

These questions were getting ridiculous and creepy. "Mr. Lundgaard, I have to be honest; I'm not comfortable with this line of questioning. So, if you don't mind, I'd rather not talk. I appreciate the ride and I don't mean to come off as ungrateful, but please, I don't feel like discussing the personal details of my life with you."

"I admire your honesty. If you don't want to talk, that's fine, just listen because I have plenty to say. First off, my name is Blaise. Not Mr. Lundgaard. Use it." He reached over and grasped her chin, forcing her to face him. Kaia let out a gasp as she read something in his blazing blue eyes. Determination. Once her gaze was locked with his, she couldn't look away even though she desperately wanted to. He released her chin, but not before he grazed her jawline with his knuckles.

Kaia flinched away.

Blaise twisted his lips into the smirk Kaia was beginning to despise. "In business, I've learned to be aggressive. Go for what I want or else lose out to someone else. I've grown accustomed to getting what I want. Since you are a woman who prefers plain speaking, I'll be frank with you. I want you, Kaia Benson."

She recoiled as if he'd struck her. At that first meeting she was hoping she'd only imagined the insinuations, but there was no denying this. "In case you haven't forgotten, "Mr. *Lundgaard*, I'm not interested or available."

"I like your spirit, Kaia. It will make it all the more interesting when I finally have you beneath me."

Her face flamed with rage. "You are disgusting." She leaned forward and tapped on the partition window.

The driver lowered the divider. "Yes?"

"Stop the car! Now! I want to get out." Kaia practically yelled wanting to get as far away from this despicable man as she possibly could.

"Sir?" the driver asked his employer.

"Keep driving until we reach our destination. And don't lower this privacy screen again, unless I specifically ask you to."

"Yes, sir." The screen went back up.

Kaia was seething. She refused to be deterred, however. As soon as the car stopped at a traffic light she tried to unlock the door to get out, but Blaise reached over and grabbed her wrist. "Let me go!"

He relaxed his grip but didn't completely let her go. "As you'll notice, that door won't unlock unless the driver presses the button on his console, and he will do no such thing unless I instruct him to. Sit back, Kaia. We'll arrive at our destination soon enough."

It occurred to her that he hadn't given the driver her address. A cold chill raced down her spine. "We're not going to my apartment, are we?"

"That's what I like about you, Kaia. You're very perceptive."

"This is kidnapping."

"Oh, I don't think so. I'm sure you'll be more than willing to stay where you are when you hear what I have to say."

She snorted, "I seriously doubt it."

He offered her a lop-sided grin. "I love a challenge."

"You're sick."

"Perhaps. Anyway, what I was getting at earlier and what you've so vehemently pointed out, you love Campion. And from what I gather, Campion loves his dance troupe. I don't mean to imply that he doesn't have feelings for you. I'm quite sure he does as any red-blooded male would be hard pressed not to. But ask yourself this, Kaia, what do you think would happen if he lost his largest financial backer?"

"You wouldn't."

"As I said, I'm a man who goes after what he wants. And I want you, Kaia. And, I mean to have you."

Chapter Four

It took every ounce of willpower that Blaise possessed not to pull Kaia close to him and claim her as he wanted to. He kept his hands firmly clenched in his lap. She continued to stare out the window, refusing to look in his direction. He had no false sense of modesty and was well aware that women found him attractive. Coupled with his extreme wealth, he was never short of bed partners. Blaise had become accustomed to women chasing him even though he preferred to be the one in pursuit, so this was a novelty to him.

He hadn't known Kaia for long, but what he had discovered about her had intrigued him and he was looking forward to getting to know her better. Shortly before he decided to become an investor in her lover's dance company, he'd had her investigated. He wanted to know everything about her from her past to what her favorite color was.

Obsessed

Kaia Benson, twenty-three years old, was raised by her mother after her father left for another woman. After the divorce was final, Darren Benson went on to marry Maryanne George, with whom he had two children. The files indicated that while he had been ordered to pay child support for Kaia's upkeep, there was no evidence that he had any further relationship with Kaia. Cynthia Benson, Kaia's mother never remarried and from what Blaise gathered, she worked hard to support herself and her daughter, who showed an aptitude for dance early on.

Kaia attended several dance workshops and programs throughout her grade school years. Before her graduation, Cynthia had fallen ill with breast cancer. In the meantime, Kaia was accepted at The Juilliard School of Arts on a full scholarship. Her mother went into remission for a year only for the cancer to return even more aggressive. Cynthia lived long enough to see her daughter graduate college.

Kaia had been dating Landon Campion, a stellar up and comer in the dance world, for the past three years. Campion had started his own company because it was said he wanted to see his own vision come to life rather than working to make someone else's happen. He made Kaia his principal dancer upon her graduation, even though she'd been offered spots in a few of the world's top dance troupes. It seemed to speak of Kaia's devotion to Campion that she would give up such lucrative opportunities when it was clear her natural abilities and talent were enough to make her a world-renowned star. From what he could gather, she was very loyal.

Blaise liked that about her. Loyalty was a trait that he found lacking among many who ran in his circles. He had no doubt that if he were to ever go bankrupt, that Lisbeth would turn her back on him. Kaia, however, seemed like the type of woman who would stick by her man in any circumstance.

The fact that she volunteered her time to give free dance lessons to disadvantaged children also spoke of her charity. He'd witnessed it firsthand upon seeing Kaia interact with his sister. At the party he'd thrown at his penthouse for the troupe, he'd casually asked the other dancers what they thought about her. The vast majority of them sang her praises. Many of them mentioned how she went out of her way to help out where she could. There were a couple of dancers who weren't as effusive in their praise but Blaise gathered it was due to jealousy. It, of course, was to be expected when someone like Kaia was involved. Some stars just shined brighter than others and there were people who didn't handle that well.

The more he learned about this precious gem, the more he wanted her, which made him more determined than ever to make her his. There was a small part of Blaise that told him that what he was doing was wrong, but with being so close to her, inhaling her scent, burning on the inside to feel her body against him, all reason flew out the window.

Since he could remember, he'd clawed his way to the top to get to the point where he was today and that didn't happen by taking no for an answer. What he wanted, he took and he wanted this woman more than he wanted air to breathe. It didn't matter that she was currently involved with another man. That could be easily resolved. Besides, Campion seemed to care more about his dance troupe than he did about Kaia.

Blaise had casually observed them together. While it was true that Kaia seemed enamored of her beau, it appeared to be more of a hero worship thing than actual love. And as for Campion, Blaise was sure the other man felt some affection toward Kaia, but it was most likely because she fed into his ego. Kaia was, after all, the most talented dancer in that troupe. She could probably be much bigger than she was now.

Seeing the two of them together had erased any doubt about his pursuit of the lovely dancer. Campion would have the backing he so desperately needed and Blaise would get Kaia. The way Blaise saw it, it was a win-win situation.

Now, all he'd have to do was get Kaia on board. He was sure she would warm up to him eventually. Though he didn't think Kaia was a gold digger, she was still a woman. Women liked to know that their men could take care of them and he was more than capable of it. Blaise was confident that once she got a taste of his lifestyle rather than slumming it with Campion, she'd realize she preferred his company.

He felt the sudden need to see her face, instead of her profile which she stubbornly continued to offer him as she stared out the window. "Whatever it is you're looking at out the window, must be very interesting."

Kaia ignored him, remaining silent and not moving an inch.

"You do realize, you can't continue to give me the silent treatment, especially when we get to our destination."

"I never asked for this ride. You're welcome to stop this car and let me out," she finally spoke but kept her gaze firmly focused on the window.

He chuckled, loving this game of cat and mouse. It had been ages since he'd actually had to work at getting a woman's interest. "Now, what would be the fun in that?"

She released a heavy sigh before finally turning in her seat to face him. Fire blazed within the depths of her dark soulful eyes. "Maybe you get a kick out of playing with people's lives because you have more money than morals but this is my life you're playing with. Whatever you think you're doing, just stop it! I'm not interested in you and I never will be, so how about we end this stupid game and part ways now?"

He raised a brow. Though her words were full of venom, he wasn't upset by them. In fact, he found them amusing. Her spunk was yet another thing that excited him about her. "Is that what you really want?"

"Yes," she practically hissed the word. She glared at him with a narrowed gaze.

Blaise chuckled softly. "Have it your way." He produced a smartphone from the breast pocket of his jacket and punched in a series of numbers.

"What are you doing?" Kaia asked, her voice full of suspicion.

"Giving you what you want."

"Hello? Mr. Lundgaard?" Campion answered on the other end. It was clear from his tone that he was surprised by the call. Blaise usually ran all his business communications through his secretary first.

"Yes. I'll cut to the chase, Campion. I'm having second thoughts about my investment." He made sure to keep his gaze locked on Kaia as he delivered the news to her lover. With a smile, Blaise pressed the speaker button so she could hear Campion's response.

"What? I thought you were pleased with the way things were run. You said I had free reign with the finances. Is there something that happened since our last meeting? Maybe we can work something out."

Kaia shook her head back and forth. Stop it, she mouthed the words.

"Listen, Campion, I'll need to get back to you. I'll be in touch." Blaise clicked off before the other man could respond.

"You, asshole! Why did you do that? Now, he's going to worry himself sick. What the hell is wrong with you?"

"I'm just showing you that I'm not the kind of man to make idle threats. My backing of Campion's little dance troupe depends on you, my dear, Kaia."

She shook her head. "You think because you have money you can just play with people's lives like this? You have no idea how hard Landon has worked to make his dream a reality. He had the backing of several other investors until you ran them off. Now you're trying to pull back, all because I'm not interested in playing your sick little game. Fuck you! I don't even understand why you'd bother offering to back Bodies in Motion in the first place if you could just pull away so easily."

"I did it because of you."

She opened her mouth but no words were forthcoming.

"At a loss for words, I see. Listen, Kaia. I can appreciate the art of dance as well as any other person. I realize how physically taxing it can be and I can also recognize when someone is good at what they do. But, dance is something I can take or leave. The only reason I even went to that festival in Copenhagen was because my sister asked me to take her, which I kindly obliged. And then, I saw you. When I watched you move across the stage as if you were made of pure magic, I was determined to have you and if that meant making you beholden to me, then so be it. I would prefer that it didn't have to come to this but I would rather you not call my bluff because I'd hate for this little dance company of yours to disband for lack of funding."

"You're a monster," she finally whispered.

He shrugged, unaffected. "I've been called worse."

Kaia began to shake and her eyes gleamed with the suspicious sheen of tears. The last thing Blaise had wanted was to upset her, but he told himself that she would eventually get over it. If he had his way, Campion would soon be a distant memory.

Kaia wanted to be sick. If she refused him, then she wasn't sure what would happen to Bodies in Motion. Even with backing, the company had struggled and then Blaise Lundgaard had come along and their money problems seemed to vanish just like that. She should have known, however, that it was too good to be true.

She couldn't deny that Blaise was a good-looking man, although that was by far an understatement, she was in love with Landon. How could she betray him for someone who just wanted to use her for his own amusement? But then again, how could she not do something when the troupe meant so much to so many people? People's livelihoods depended on it.

"So, what exactly are you asking me?"

He took her hand which she immediately tried to snatch away but he tightened his grip. "I expect you to be mine in every sense of the word. You'll be my hostess and companion." The emphasis he placed on that last word left no doubt in her mind about what he wanted.

She gasped at the intensity of his lustful gaze. It sent a shiver up her spine. Kaia shook her head to rid it of any thought that led her to wonder what being with him would be like. He repulsed her and she wanted nothing to do with him and his heavy-handed tactics. She yanked her hand away with all her might, this time successful in breaking loose. "I suppose that includes sharing your bed."

A half smile tilted his lips. "It would be our bed, Kaia. Everything I own would be yours."

"I don't want anything from you other to than to be left alone. I'm not a whore who'll sleep around just because some wealthy man decides he wants to throw money at me."

"I know you're not a whore. They bore me. You, on the other hand, I doubt I'd ever get tired of you." His grin widened.

She wanted to punch him right in his perfect teeth. "I'm not just going to jump into bed with you."

"And, I don't expect you to. I'm not an unreasonable man. I'd like for us to get to know each other better. And when you're comfortable...we'll see where that leads us."

"The only place I'd like to go with you is to a cliff so I can push you off of it. You are absolutely insane. Do you make a habit of blackmailing women into being with you?"

He shrugged his shoulder with obvious nonchalance. "What you call blackmail, I'd call a starting point of the negotiation." He patted her knee causing her to flinch. "Relax Kaia, I'll give you some time to sort things out. In the meantime, sit back and enjoy the ride. We'll be at our destination shortly."

She scooted as far away from him as she could and averted her gaze to the window, not looking at anything in particular. Kaia had heard about people like him before. People who were so callous with others when it came to getting what they wanted that they stopped at nothing to get what they wanted. It scared her shitless that she was the object of his misguided obsession.

She was so deep in thought, she didn't realize the car had stopped.

"We're here," Blaise mentioned casually.

Her door was opened by the driver and she was tempted to push past him and run away. Instead, she slid out of the car and waited for Blaise. She was numb. Unsure of what to do as he guided her through a parking lot and up an elevator. It suddenly occurred to her where she was. At his place.

"No." She backed away from him.

"Take it easy, my dear. Like I said, I'll give you some time to ponder my proposition. Besides, we won't be alone."

She didn't have a chance to ask him what he meant when he practically pushed her inside. The sound of loud pop music blasted around the penthouse. Aneka wheeled around the living room to the rhythm. Her eyes were shut tight and she seemed to be lost in the sound that surrounded her.

Blaise marched across the room and picked up a small remote control and pressed a button that shut the music off. Aneka opened her eyes.

"Blaise! *Jeg havde ikke forventet dig hjem så tidligt.*"

"English please, Aneka. We have company." He glanced in Kaia's direction. "And, of course, I didn't tell you I would be home so early because I wanted to surprise you."

The girl turned to see Kaia standing by the door and her face lit up. She wheeled her chair over to Kaia. "You came! I wasn't sure when I would see you again."

Kaia had every intention of keeping her promise and visiting Aneka again, but she didn't appreciate being strong-armed into it by Blaise. "I told you I'd come by for a visit."

"I'm so glad you're here. You saw me dancing. I must have looked foolish in my chair." Aneka blushed.

"You looked great."

Aneka giggled. "You're just being nice, but that's okay. I'd really like to show you my room if you have the time."

"Of course, she does," Blaise interjected. "In fact, I have a feeling Kaia will be spending a lot of time with us in the future."

Bastard.

Chapter Five

"This is my vision board. I like to cut out pictures from magazines and pin them here along with keepsakes and other items that help me stay motivated. Those are the tickets to the Festival where I first saw you dance." Aneka pointed to a large corkboard hanging on her wall with various images of dancers. There were pictures of celebrities and people running, theater stubs and pieces of ribbon.

Kaia stared at the board politely and smiled. She wished she could be more enthusiastic about what she was being shown, but she couldn't get her mind off the fact that Blaise was willing to destroy Bodies in Motion in order to get what he wanted. Her.

It made her sick to her stomach at how casually he could ruin another person's life on a whim. Part of her was creeped out that he'd go to such lengths to be with her, but on the other hand, Kaia couldn't help but feel a little flattered that a man of Blaise's caliber would want her. Surely, someone like him would want someone who was more suitable for his lifestyle, more sophisticated, a woman who could move easily within the circles he was probably a part of. Blaise had the status and looks to have world-renowned beauties on his arm.

Kaia wasn't Quasimodo but she certainly didn't put herself in the category of some of the stunners she imagined would be better suited for Blaise. Not that any of it mattered, anyway. She loved Landon and had since the moment she'd met him. Landon was talented and driven and she admired his vision. This was all a game to Blaise and she refused to be his toy.

"What do you think Kaia?"

Kaia realized that Aneka had still been talking. She turned her attention to the young girl and smiled. "I uh...think that's great."

Aneka clasped her hands together. "That's wonderful. I'll tell Blaise."

"Tell Blaise what?"

"That you're having dinner with us. He'll be very pleased."

"Wait a minute. I'm sorry. But I already have plans tonight. I misspoke."

"Oh." The look of disappointment on Aneka's face tore at her Kaia's heart. She wished she had been paying attention.

"I'll tell you what, maybe the two of us can go out for a bite one night. It can be a girl's night out."

"Oh, I'd really love that. I wish you could stay with us tonight. The chef is making my favorite. It's a pasta dish with seafood."

"Perhaps, you'd consider changing your mind. There would be plenty to eat. Our chef cooks more than enough for Aneka and myself." Blaise entered the room with a smug grin tilting his lips.

Kaia narrowed her gaze. She wanted to punch him in his supercilious face but she didn't want to upset Aneka. "As I was telling your sister, I have plans tonight."

"Aw, yes. With your friend, Campion. Am I correct?"

"Yes. I'm supposed to have a night out with my *boyfriend*. I'm already late getting home and he's probably wondering where I am."

His grin widened. "I don't know about that. Considering, he's called my phone several times in the past hour. I'd venture to guess that he's more concerned about our conversation from earlier."

"You..."

He raised a brow. "You what?"

Kaia stole a glance in Aneka's direction. The child looked back and forth between her and Blaise with a look of bewilderment stamped on her face. "You shouldn't have done that. I need to call him."

"By all means. Do that. Invite him over for dinner. I'm sure he wouldn't mind changing his plans when you tell him where you are."

It was almost like he'd had this planned. What did Blaise possibly think he could accomplish by having Landon over?

Aneka clapped her hands with glee. "Oh, that would be great if Mr. Campion could join us for dinner as well."

Blaise smirked. "You see, Kaia? He's more than welcome and you wouldn't want to disappoint Aneka, would you? After all, she is the biggest fan of your Bodies in Motion." While his words were innocuous, the underlying threat was still there.

Kaia took a deep breath to keep herself from cursing this man out. She didn't want to lose her cool in front of Aneka, who was probably unaware that her brother was a douchebag. "Fine. If you two will excuse me, I'm going to step out into the hallway to make that call."

Blaise nodded. "You do that."

When Kaia tried to walk out of the room, however, Blaise blocked the door in a way that made it impossible for her to move past him without touching. She tilted her head back in order to glare at him. "Excuse me. I need to get by."

"Of course." He moved a few inches to the side forcing her to brush against him.

Kaia twisted her body to have as little contact with him as possible but as she slid by, Blaise moved closer, causing her breast to graze his arm.

"Asshole," she muttered under her breath.

His soft chuckled taunted her as she successfully made it to the hallway. If Aneka wasn't around, she would have kicked him in the nuts. After putting some distance between herself and Aneka's room, Kaia pulled out her phone and saw that she had five missed calls from Landon. She'd forgotten to turn the sound back on her phone when she'd left the recreation center. She hit the button to automatically dial Landon's number.

"Where are you?" were the first words out of his mouth.

"Hello, to you, too, Landon."

He sighed. "I'm not in the mood to play word games. I'm extremely stressed right now and you were supposed to be home an hour ago. You could have at least texted me to let me know you were running late."

That call from Blaise must have really gotten to Landon because she could hear the upset in his voice. "I'm sorry. I'm actually at Mr. Lundgaard's place. He happened to see me walking to the subway and offered me a ride."

"What? You're with him now?"

"Yes, his sister wanted me to stay for dinner. Actually, that's why I'm calling. They wanted me to invite you over. I know we're supposed to go out tonight and I can tell them no and come home but—"

"No! Stay right where you are. I can be over there in a half hour. I'll get a taxi. Did he happen to mention anything about pulling his support from the dance company?"

Kaia wasn't sure what to say. Her boyfriend was upset enough as it was. How would he feel if he knew what Blaise Lundgaard had in mind for her? "Um...he might have mentioned something."

"You know something, don't you? Never mind. I'll talk to him about it when I arrive. I'm leaving the apartment now. See you when I get there."

"But Landon—"

He hung up before she could finish.

"Dammit," she muttered under her breath. All she could foresee from his visit was a disaster. Landon would be devastated when he learned the truth.

"Trouble?"

Kaia nearly jumped out of her skin at the unexpected sound of Blaise's voice. She whirled around and shot him a narrowed eye stare. "Could you, please, not sneak up on me like that?"

He raised a brow. "I beg your pardon, Kaia. I didn't mean to frighten you. I only wanted to check on you and see if all was well."

"Landon will be over within the hour if that's what you wanted to know."

"That wasn't what I was asking actually." He moved toward her, his eyes were predatory as he neared.

"Then what are you asking?"

"Did you tell him?"

"Of course not. How the hell am I supposed to break the news to him that you're threatening to take away all that he's worked for just because you want to sleep with me?"

His lips tilted into a sinister grin. "As you get to know me, sweet Kaia, you'll learn I don't make threats. I make promises." He held her stare until he was only inches away from her. He gently brushed the side of her face with the back of his hand.

She flinched away, disgusted with herself for letting him get too close. "Don't touch me."

"Why not? I like touching you, Kaia. I'd very much like to do it, again." He was the Big Bad Wolf and she was Little Red, and he stared down at her like she was a tasty treat.

Kaia took a step back but he advanced. So, she took another and he followed in what became a slow chase. She desperately eyed the stairs but much to her frustration, she'd have to get past him in order to make it down. "Uh, looks like Aneka may need some assistance."

Blaise turned his head to look behind him. Taking advantage of his momentary distraction, she pushed past him and ran down the stairs. Not caring that she left her bag behind, she headed for the door determined to get out of this penthouse and away from that demon. What she didn't count on was a man of his size being so swift. By the time she made it to the door, Blaise caught up to her capturing her by the waist and pulling Kaia against him. He then pressed her against the door, keeping her trapped with the full weight of his body.

"Let me go," she hissed, trying to wiggle her way out of the hold he had on her.

Blaise bent his head until his lips nearly touched her earlobe. "Never. Didn't anyone ever tell you that when you run, it only makes a man want to chase you? Pretty clever of you, using my sister's name in your attempt to escape."

"Don't you understand that I don't want this? Don't want you? This is wrong and creepy. I just want to be left alone." The more she fought to free herself, the more confined she felt. Tears of frustration stung her eyes.

"Why fight the inevitable, little one? You will be mine."

"You are an entitled asshole and I want nothing to do with you. If it weren't for that sweet little girl upstairs, I'd stab you in the chest but unfortunately, you're all she has. And for some reason, she thinks you're a decent human being."

He captured her earlobe between his teeth and gave it a sharp nip. She gasped. "That's one of the things I like about you, Kaia, your spirit." He pressed a very large erection against her rear. "See what you do to me? No woman has ever made me want her the way you have."

"I haven't made you do anything. You're just playing some sick game with me that I want no part of. Please don't do this. Landon has worked so hard to create Bodies in Motion. He's poured in so much of his own money that if production ends this will ruin him financially, not to mention it would crush his spirit to see his hard work go down the drain. I'm begging you, Mr. Lundgaard. Please leave us alone. I'll be a companion to your sister or whatever else you want me to do but I can't be your...plaything."

To Kaia's surprise, he released an impatient growl and whirled her around until she was facing him. He lowered his head until he was nose to nose with her. "My name is Blaise. Say it or I'll kiss off every bit of that lip gloss that's been tempting me since I saw you earlier."

She pressed her hands against his chest in an attempt to push him away. "Stop!"

"Say my name, Kaia."

"Blaise! Okay? Are you happy?"

He smiled. "Not quite, but I will be when you're saying my name in the throes of passion." He backed away from her then.

"You're a twisted man. Your sick fantasy is never going to happen."

"Never say never, little one."

"Stop calling me that. Don't you understand what the word 'no' means? Having a lot of money doesn't give you the right to anything you want and that includes me."

"Everything and everyone has a price, my dear. Everyone."

"Not me."

"Oh, I bet you do, too. It's just not obvious, yet."

"You must have mistaken me for someone else. I just don't understand why you would pursue someone who obviously has no interest in you."

Blaise raised a brow. "Oh? So, we're going to ignore the heat coming from your body when I held you against me or the way your nipples have tightened under your t-shirt. You may deny it, little one, but you're attracted to me. Campion is a boy and he can't satisfy you the way you deserve."

Kaia crossed her arms over her chest, mainly to cover her breasts. She attributed the sudden rise in her body heat to her anger. There was no possible way that she wanted this man. Sure, he was good looking and most women would find him sexy. But, she found his arrogance a turn-off and the fact that he was trying to blackmail her into sleeping with him was despicable. "And I suppose you can?"

"Should I put it to the test?"

"No!"

His grin widened. "You're so adorable when you're in denial, but there's no need to panic, little one. At least for now. When you come to me, you will be willing. And, you will love it. Why don't you go back upstairs to my sister? I'll wait down here for Campion to arrive." This time, when Blaise moved out of the way, he gave her wide berth.

Kaia rushed past him without looking back. She saw no point in arguing with him. The man was insane if he thought she would willingly be with him. When Landon arrived, he'd tell that bastard off and they could finally have him out of their lives. Sure, it would be a huge loss for the company to not have Blaise's backing but Kaia believed in Landon. He was a hard worker and a visionary. He'd find a way out of this mess. He just had to!

For the next hour, it was difficult to sit with Aneka and pretend everything was okay. She was half listening to the girl as she rambled on about any and everything. Kaia thought that Aneka was a sweetheart but the nonstop chatter was frazzling her nerves. By the time Landon arrived, she was so on edge, the slightest annoyance would have set Kaia off.

Dinner was another ordeal in itself. Landon was just as tense as she was. Aneka continued to talk while Blaise put on a good show of acting as though he didn't have their livelihoods in the palm of his hand. He drank wine and smiled indulgently at his sister and discussed mundane topics like the weather.

By the time dessert rolled around, Kaia felt like screaming.

"Aneka, if you'd please excuse us, there's an important business matter I'd like to discuss with Landon and Kaia."

Aneka sighed. "Okay. I'm going up to my room. Make sure you call the serviceman tomorrow to fix the elevator. It's been a little slow for me lately."

"Of course. I'll make that call first thing in the morning."

Aneka turned to Kaia's direction. "Kaia, will you come by my room before you leave?"

Kaia managed to smile. "Sure."

"Okay. I'll leave you adults to your business conversation." With a final wave, she rolled out of the dining room.

Landon turned to Kaia. "Why don't you join, Aneka? If we're discussing the company's financial status, you don't have to be present."

"On the contrary, Campion, Kaia's presence is very much necessary. After all, it's up to her whether I withdraw my backing or not."

Landon turned to her. "What is he talking about Kaia?"

She glared in Blaise's direction. "Don't do this."

"Don't do what?" Landon demanded.

"Would you like to enlighten him, Kaia? Or should I?" Blaise took a sip from his wineglass.

"Would someone please tell me what's going on?" Landon demanded, expounding on his words with a pound of his fist to the table.

How was she supposed to look her boyfriend in the eye and tell him that he would lose everything he worked for just because some psycho wanted to sleep with her? She looked down at her lap unable to meet Landon's gaze.

"Campion, as you can imagine, a man in my position doesn't get where he is without taking what he wants. But sometimes in order to get what we want, we have to give a little something in return. I believe it's called *quid pro quo*. I admire your drive and I'm willing to back your little dance troupe. In fact, I'm willing to double the amount I initially promised."

Landon grinned. "Wow, Mr. Lundgaard. That's great!" But just as fast as his smile appeared, it disappeared. "Wait. There's a catch, isn't there?"

Blaise raised his glass. "*Quid pro quo.*"

"If you want more of a return on your investment, we can work something out I'm sure," Landon said slowly.

"You can have all the money. I don't need a return on my investment. The money would be yours to do as you will."

Landon looked at Kaia and then back at Blaise. "So, what do you want in return?"

"I want Kaia. And let me make this perfectly clear to you, so there'll be no misunderstanding. I don't want her for just one night. I want her to be mine in every capacity of the word."

Kaia couldn't take any more of this. She stood up. "This is ridiculous. Landon, the man is obviously deranged. There's no way, I'm going to be with him and I'm sure you wouldn't even consider such a ridiculous proposition."

Landon to her surprise, however, seemed to actually be considering this's nut's proposal. "For how long?"

If Blaise Lundgaard's crazy offer wasn't enough to take the wind out of her sails, Landon's casual question was a shot in the heart.

Obsessed

Kaia couldn't get out of the penthouse fast enough. After pushing away from the table, she grabbed her bag that she'd left in the living room and headed out the door. Tears blinded her as she made her way out of the building. She was nearly hit by a car as she ran across the street. She vaguely registered an angry motorist screaming obscenities at her as she thankfully reached the subway unscathed.

By the time she made it back to the loft she shared with Landon, Kaia was a mess. She went into her bedroom and collapsed on the bed. Tears streamed down her face as it occurred to her that not only was Landon considering Blaise's crazy plan, but the fact that he didn't bother coming after her.

Had she been a fool all these years to devote herself to a man who clearly didn't care for her as much as she believed he did? That he would even consider throwing away everything they'd shared for the past three years for money was enough to make her want to throw up. Kaia had been certain Landon would cuss that arrogant asshole out, and perhaps punch him. But there hadn't been the slightest hesitation.

There were a few dancers in the troupe who intimated that Landon wasn't as into Kaia as much as she was into him. Kaia had always brushed that off as jealousy but now she wondered. The very fact that he didn't come after her another indicator that he didn't seem to give a damn.

Chapter Six

When the front door closed with a decisive bang, Blaise watched Campion's reaction carefully. The other man glanced over his shoulder and turned back to him with uncertainty clouding his gaze. "Maybe I should go after her," he offered weakly.

Any respect Blaise might have had for Landon Campion evaporated at that moment. What kind of man was he to allow another man to proposition his woman and then do nothing about it? And then seeing said woman was in distress still not react? Blaise didn't care that he was the man doing the propositioning, he actually expected the other man to at least put up some form of token protest, but there had been absolutely nothing.

At least, now Blaise knew that the relationship Kaia had been desperately fighting to save had obviously one-sided. He'd seen Campion's type before, ambitious to a fault. But, it was the kind of ambition that gave way to greed. He was certain the Campion would sell his own mother if the opportunity presented itself.

Blaise didn't bother to respond to the other man. Instead, he took a sip from his wine glass and returned his attention to his meal. He felt like making the other man squirm, because of the obvious pain he'd inflicted on Kaia and mainly because he could.

"Mr. Lundgaard...I don't know what to say. I must apologize for Kaia's behavior. She gets emotional sometimes. I'm sure she must have misunderstood what it is you want out of this."

Blaise took his time chewing and swallowing before responding. "Oh, she didn't misunderstand. I've already spoken to her at length about exactly what I want."

Campion's brow shot up. "And exactly what is it you want from her? She did mention something about visiting your little sister from time to time."

Blaise smirked. "Among other things."

"Like what?"

"When I previously brought my proposal to you, offering financial backing for your dance company, I took you to be a shrewd man with at least average intelligence. So please don't insult mine by pretending that you don't know exactly what I'm talking about."

Campion turned a deep shade of red and squirmed in his seat. "It's just that... I mean this can't be real life, right? What do you want with Kaia? You can have any woman you want. Why her?"

"Why not her? You're her current beau so do you even need an answer to that question." Blaise took another sip of his wine and watched the other man from over the rim.

"Well, I mean, I know why I'm dating her but a man like you could have any woman he wants. Beautiful, classy women."

As each second passed, Landon Campion became a bigger piece of shit. Blaise could feel anger rumbled in his chest. He already considered Kaia his and to hear another man dismiss her attributes so casually pissed him off.

"Since you're so curious why I want her and will have her, by the way, I shall enlighten you. When I see all that silky brown skin and those tempting curves, it makes me want to run my hands all over her body. She has the face of an angel and when she smiles, it's like receiving your own little piece of heaven. She moves like dance was created specifically for her. And her passion shines through everything she does from her dancing to her teaching disadvantaged children and her misguided loyalty to people who clearly don't deserve it." Blaise paused to make sure Campion knew that the last comment was directed at him.

The other man squirmed one again. Spineless punk.

"And I'm sure that passion would translate to more...adult activities."

"So, you just want to use her for sex."

Blaise chuckled. "How very pedestrian of you. For a man of vision as I've heard you described, you have a very limited view when it comes to your partner. To hear you talk, one would be correct in assuming that you don't love her."

"I do love Kaia, it's just none of this makes sense to me. You've gone to extraordinary lengths for one woman when there are literally millions who would come running if you snapped your fingers."

Blaise leaned back in his chair and narrowed his gaze as he stared at his rival. "I'm what one would call a cynic. Some would say I'm not a nice person and I can accept that. The world is full of bullshitters, con artists and malcontents and it is my very special gift to be able to see through them. But all is not dark. There are a handful of people who simply carry within them a light. And Kaia is one of those people. Call me selfish if you'd like, but I want her light all to myself."

"So, you see, I might be able to have any woman I want as you so delicately put it, but in my opinion, no other woman compares to Kaia. What I find so surprising is that you're not willing to fight for her. After all, when I invited the dancers of Bodies of Motion over here, the two of you seemed quite lovey-dovey. Was I wrong to assume your relationship isn't as serious as I believed?"

It seemed as if Campion was at a loss for words. His mouth opened and then closed as if he was fishing for the right words. "Well, we were, I mean, are. I do love Kaia, but what makes you think she'd go along with this?"

"Because if I don't I on withdrawing financial backing from your company. Kaia may resist at first but when she sees things for what they are she'll give in."

Campion lost all color, his face going white as a sheet. "So, what...you're going to force yourself on her?"

"Something tells me even if that were the case you wouldn't give a shit, as long as you got what you wanted."

"That's not true!" Campion smashed his fist against the table.

"As Hamlet's mother once said, 'The lady doth protests too much."

The other man jumped to his feet. "I'm not going to stand here and be insulted."

"Sit down, Campion."

Campion glared at him, remaining on his feet defiantly.

"Fine. Obviously, you're not as shrewd as I believed you to be and I don't do business with petulant children. You may see yourself out of my home." Blaise picked up his wine glass and took a healthy gulp.

Campion turned to leave but stopped. Slowly, he turned around. "So, you won't invest in Bodies in Motion?

Blaise would laugh in his face if this scenario wasn't so predictable.

"No. Good evening, Mr. Campion."

"But—"

"I said, good evening."

"Wait. I mean...I don't see why we couldn't work something out. I mean, you wouldn't hurt her, would you?"

Blaise tightened his hand around the stem of his glass to the point where it nearly broke but he managed to restrain himself. As far as he was concerned, he was doing Kaia a favor by getting her away from this opportunist. "I wouldn't make her do anything she didn't want."

"Well, then...let's talk."

Blaise smirked. He had Campion right where he wanted him and soon the same would be said for the lovely Ms. Benson.

She wasn't sure how long she lay on the bed, but as each hour passed, the angrier she grew. Where the hell was he? Surely, dinner was over a while ago. And whatever 'business' Landon and Blaise had to discuss couldn't possibly take this long.

Kaia must have dozed off because she awoke to the sound of the bedroom door opening. It was dark so she peered at the clock on the nightstand. It was nearly midnight! She turned on the lamp which illuminated the room.

Landon froze as if he'd gotten caught with his hand in the proverbial cookie jar. "Kaia…I didn't mean to wake you."

"Gee, how considerate of you." She rolled her eyes and slid off the bed. She wasn't sure if she wanted to scream at him or hit him.

"It's late, so maybe we can talk in the morning."

She noticed how he wouldn't make eye contact with her. "What's there to talk about Landon? That you're willing to pimp me out to save the dance troupe or that you didn't bother to come after me when I was clearly upset. I don't understand how you could be so calm about everything when that…that egomaniac offered you that ridiculous proposal."

Landon ran his fingers through his hair. "This is too heavy a conversation to get into right now. Can we just sleep on it? And, discuss it in the morning?"

How could he be so nonchalant about this entire situation? Part of her had hoped when he came home he'd say something to put her mind at ease. But the longer the silence lengthened between them, the more hope she lost that whatever they had between them could be salvaged. Kaia had thought she was all cried out but tears sprang to her eyes.

"What did you talk about after I left?"

"Kaia…listen, I love you okay." Again, he wouldn't make eye contact.

"What did you talk about?" she repeated more forcefully.

"You're getting hysterical. Let's talk about this when cooler heads prevail."

"What did you talk about?" she screamed.

Landon turned his back to her. "His company has an endowment fund to the tune of five million dollars a year. A sum like that is generally spread out across several programs. He's willing to send two million of it our way. We've never had a contribution that large. We could do so much with that money. We could pay the dancers what they're worth, we could recruit more talent. We could invest the money and get a great return. The troupe could operate in the black for years to come without any financial burdens."

Kaia wiped away a stray tear that slid down her cheek. "You keep saying 'we' as if I'm actually being consulted on this grand scheme of yours. I already told you how I felt about this mess. But, you're basically telling me that you're willing to sell me off for this money and all these grand ideas you have."

Landon turned to face her with a heavy sigh. "I'm not selling you off, Kaia. Look, I had a long talk with Mr. Lundgaard. He said he wouldn't make you do anything you didn't want to. All you'd have to do is play hostess and hang out with his sister."

Kaia blinked a few times because she was certain she'd somehow landed in the Twilight Zone. She couldn't figure out if Landon was deliberately being obtuse or if he was really that stupid. "You're kidding me, right? I don't have to do anything I don't want to? Really? Because I don't want to have anything to fucking do with that man."

"Kaia, think of the big picture. Just play hostess for a little while and eventually, he'll get bored of the whole thing and move on to someone else. I mean, it would be arrogant of you to think you'd be able to hold his attention for long."

Landon could have said a number of things to her at that moment, but none of them would have hurt quite as much as what he'd just said. It was as if the last three years meant absolutely nothing to him.

Kaia walked over to the bed and sat down. She saw no point in screaming or arguing. It was clear that her relationship was over. How could she be with someone who wasn't willing to fight for her, and worst yet, thought so little of her? It felt as if her heart was breaking into tiny pieces. But the man she loved, couldn't be bothered to tell her that everything would be all right and that they'd find some other way to save the dance troupe. He could barely make eye contact.

As the silence lengthened between them, a numbness washed over her. Kaia finally lifted her head to look at Landon, who she was seeing with new eyes. Could it possibly be that her admiration and love for him had made her see something in him that wasn't there? He shifted back and forth, looking uncomfortable as hell. He rubbed the back of his head, something he did when he was nervous about something.

"If you don't go through with this, we lose the backing and we might as well kiss the troupe goodbye. All the dancers and technicians will be out of work. I mean in a way this is kind of your fault. If Lundgaard wasn't so fixated on you, we'd be doing just fine. I mean, it can't be a coincidence that we started losing backers and all of a sudden, he swoops in with this generous offer of his. Look at it this way—"

"Stop talking." She couldn't hear another word of his nonsense.

"Kaia—"

"I said, stop talking," she said with more force the second time.

The room fell quiet once more as her head spun as she tried to get a grasp of the situation. On the one hand, being anywhere near Blaise Lundgaard was something she found distasteful. But on the other hand, if she didn't go through with this, Bodies in Motion would go down in flames and the dancers, many of whom were her friends would be out of work. Dance was a competitive field and a very small percentage of dancers were able to make a full-time career of it. Would her conscience be able to handle it if the troupe went under? If she did do it, it would be for Landon's selfish ass.

"Did you ever love me?" She wasn't sure why the question was so important and perhaps in the grand scheme of things it probably didn't matter. But for her piece of mind, she needed to know.

"Of course, I did. I still do, Kaia."

"You have a funny way of showing it, Landon!"

"So, I'm just supposed to throw my dreams away? I've worked damn hard to make Bodies in Motion a success."

"And I was right there with you, as well as the rest of the dancers. Don't pretend you did this by yourself."

"But, I created it. It was my vision. My dream!" He slammed his hand against his chest to emphasize his words.

"And it's always been about you, hasn't it?"

"Of course not. I'm doing this for our future. Can't you see?"

"No, I don't see. Please enlighten me."

"As I already pointed out, you don't have to sleep with him. Just play along and we'll have his money."

Obsessed

Now that the blinders had been completely ripped off, Kaia thought of all the times she'd put Landon's needs ahead of her own. He had been the one to convince her to dance for his troupe. She'd been given a few other opportunities over the years. In fact, a huge pop star had asked Kaia to be a dancer on her world tour and it was Landon who had convinced her to turn it down. It didn't matter that it was something Kaia had wanted to do.

She'd sacrificed to keep him happy and to help him make his dream happen while ignoring her own. She'd actually convinced herself that this was where she was supposed to be because of all the things Landon had fed to her. She was just another cog in his wheel. Someone he could bend to his while and discard on a whim.

It took every ounce of self-restraint she still possessed to not get up and kick him square in the face. That he didn't see how fucked up this entire situation was, was one thing. But knowing he didn't care, was another.

She couldn't be around him right now or else she'd end up doing something that would land her in prison. Taking a deep breath, she stood up and headed to the closet to retrieve an overnight bag. There was no way she could stay here.

"What are you doing?" he asked, his voice heavy with wariness.

Kaia didn't answer as she collected a few outfits and her toiletries to pack.

Landon placed his hand on her shoulder. "You don't have to leave."

She shrugged his hand off. "Don't touch me."

He grabbed her by the arm, but she turned around and pushed him with all her might, causing him to stumble back and hit the wall. "I said, don't fucking touch me!" she screamed as she returned to her task of packing.

"You're being ridiculous, Kaia. Where are you going to go?"

"Somewhere."

"So, you're just going to leave without talking this out?"

"What's there to talk about? It's clear the two of us have two different ideas about what it takes to make a relationship work. So, what's the point of me staying?"

"And what about Bodies in Motion? You're just going to let it go under."

She couldn't believe he had the audacity to even bring that up. If she had any doubts about leaving, he'd certainly just confirmed that she had the right idea. Once she was finished packing, she grabbed her bag and headed out the bedroom. She slipped on her shoes, collected her jacket and keys and headed out the door.

Landon, however, had other ideas. He was there in an instant. He placed his palm against the door when Kaia opened it, forcing it closed again.

"Let's work this out."

"There's nothing to work out. We are done and right now, I can't stand to look at you."

"Kaia, you're being overly dramatic about this situation. You're not some heroine in some Victorian melodrama. This is real life, dammit, and we have real bills to pay. Try to see things from my perspective!"

She took several deep calming breaths before turning to face him. "I'd like to counter what you said with this..." She pushed him just enough to make him lose his balance.

Landon cried out as he toppled backward.

Obsessed

This gave Kaia enough time to get out the door. She rushed down the stairs and was out of their apartment building, not wanting to give him the chance to catch up with her. Kaia ran for two blocks, not stopping until she reached a subway station. Thankfully, she didn't have to wait long for her train. Once Kaia was seated, however, she realized she had nowhere to go.

A couple days ago, she was happy. She had a job doing something she loved, she was in love, and while things weren't always smooth sailing, Kaia had been content with her life.

And then Blaise Lundgaard came storming into her life, destroying everything with the snap of his fingers. Even if she did refuse his offer, she had a sinking feeling, in the pit of her stomach, that this was only the beginning.

Chapter Seven

When it came to matters of business, Blaise was the epitome of calm, cool and collected. It was how he'd transformed his father's company into the juggernaut it had become. But when it came to matters of a personal nature, he could be very impatient. It had been two days since he'd heard from either Campion or Kaia. He was certain after his conversation that he'd hear from at least one of them. But instead, he was left in the dark. This game of cat and mouse was slowly pushing him over the edge.

He was tempted to head down to the studio where Bodies in Motion held their practices. Drumming his fingers on his desk, his mind drifted to his last conversations with both Kaia and Campion individually. While Kaia was not yet on board, Campion certainly was. The little bastard's eyes had lit up with greed when Blaise had given him a figure he would invest. That had come with Campion's promise to talk Kaia into doing the 'right thing'. If he was correct about Kaia's reaction, that 'talk' would cause an irreparable rift between the two of them, just as he planned.

So why had things been so quiet lately?

He'd intentionally let them be these past couple days because he wanted things to simmer for a bit. With a frustrated sigh, Blaise reached for his phone but it rang before he could make his call. Glancing at the number on his caller ID, he saw that it was Campion. He let it ring a few more times before answering.

"Yes?" he answered curtly.

"Mr. Lundgaard, it's Landon Campion."

"I'm aware. But what I'm curious about, is why I'm only hearing from you now?"

"Well, there seems to be a bit of a problem..."

"Well? What is it?"

"Kaia is missing. When I went home after leaving your place, we kind of got into an argument about you. And well, she packed a bag and left."

"And you didn't stop her?"

"Short of tying her to the bed so she couldn't escape, what would you have had me do? Besides, I thought she would be back when she cooled down because most of her things are still here. But she hasn't shown up to practice these past two days and no one in the troupe has seen her."

"Why am I just hearing about this now?" Blaise roared, his temper exploding.

His outburst was briefly met with silence before Campion answered. "Well, at first, I thought she might be with you. But from the way you answered, I guess not."

"You should have called me the second she walked out the door."

"Well, it was past midnight and I didn't want to disturb you."

"Midnight? You left my penthouse a little after eight. Do you mean to tell me it took you that long to go home? You allowed her to stew for hours?"

"There was something I needed to check on at the studio and I guess I lost track of time."

Wanting to hear no more, Blaise disconnected the call. Fool! Now, he was tasked with finding Kaia and hoping she'd come to no harm in the process. While he was certain she was capable of taking care of herself, she was still a lone woman in the city. The fact that Campion and none of her friends had heard from Kaia was bothersome to him.

He immediately dialed the number of the agency that provided a security detail for him when necessary as well as some private detective work. He vowed he'd find Kaia or heads would fucking roll.

Between crying, stuffing her face with copious amounts of butter pecan ice cream and watching trashing talk shows, Kaia was an absolute mess. She rode the train for hours, not knowing where she would go. It wasn't until she noticed the rush hour crowd getting on that Kaia realized she had been on the subway for hours. She got off and found herself in the Williamsburg section of Brooklyn. She found herself on Patty's doorstep.

Patty had been surprised to see her but surprisingly didn't ask any questions. She'd been camping out on Patty's couch since then.

Obsessed

Kaia lay on the couch with the television on, although she wasn't paying attention. She stared listlessly in front of her trying not to think about how easy it was for Landon to cast her aside.

"Okay, that's it. Get up." Patty stood between her and television, hands on her hip. "You're in the same spot I left you in. Have you even showered? And did you eat another pint of my ice cream?"

With a heavy sigh, Kaia sat up. "I'm sorry. It's just..." Tears sprang to her eyes. "I'm so pathetic."

"Aww, honey," Patty flounced on the couch beside her and put her arm around her shoulder. "Whatever argument you had with Landon, I'm sure the two of you can work it out. Besides, he was going crazy when you didn't show up to rehearsal these past couple days. And since you weren't there, we had to practice the routine with Deena as the lead." Patty made a gagging sound.

Deena, who was Kaia's understudy, could be a bit of a diva at times and didn't get along with any of the other women in the troupe, preferring the company of the males. Kaia had tolerated her for the sake of harmony, but other than that she could take her or leave her.

Kaia shrugged. "It doesn't matter. I'm not sure if I'm going back to Bodies in Motion. And, Landon and I are definitely over."

"What?" Patty squawked. "I knew whatever happened between the two of you had to be major for you to come to my place in the state you were in. But a breakup? You've got to be kidding me. You two are crazy about each other."

"I thought that, too, but my eyes have been opened to a side of Landon that I simply can't abide. It's best that we make a clean break for the sake of everyone around us. I don't want there to be any unnecessary drama or awkwardness by me being around everyone else."

"Wow. So, you're just going to throw away your dream because some jackass broke your heart."

Kaia sniffed. "What do you mean?"

"I mean you're doing it, again. You're allowing him to dictate your life. I just don't understand it, Kaia!"

"What do you mean, dictate my life? I don't understand what you're talking about."

Patty sighed running her hand through a mess of red curls. "When I joined Bodies in Motion, I was thrilled because Landon has been touted as one of the soon to be greats. He'd already made quite a name for himself in the dance world. He's brilliant. But, he knows that. And then, there was you, by his side and I noticed you. Seeing you dance for the first time, was almost like a spiritual experience. You're basically like all of my favorite dancers rolled into one. But when you move, you make it look so effortless even though I know you work your ass off. Landon may be good, one of the best in fact, but he's no you. By far, you're the most talented dancer in the troupe, one of the best I've ever seen. It's why he holds you back."

Kaia furrowed her brows together at Patty's assessment. She realized she was good at what she did, but it was because she loved to dance so much. It was how she expressed herself. When her father had left Kaia and her mother, dance had been her therapy. It had helped her going through those awkward teen years and the feeling of rejection she'd experienced from the man who was supposed to love her unconditionally. Dance had helped her when her mother got sick and eventually succumbed to her illness. Dance was a part or her. To some, it was just a hobby or a job. But to her, it was everything. She needed it like oxygen.

"How do you figure he was holding me back?"

Patty rolled her eyes. "Sure, Bodies in Motion is going places and we're growing but we're still small potatoes. You were offered spots large in productions."

"Where I would have been a backup. Landon made me principal."

"The way you dance, it wouldn't have taken you long to go to the top. Besides, what about that pop star who saw the show? She wanted you to go on tour with her."

"I couldn't leave the show behind."

"But, it would have been a fantastic opportunity for you. I bet Landon somehow convinced you that those opportunities were beneath you. I could give you a handful of examples but here's one that pertains to Bodies in Motion. Why won't he allow you to choreograph more? The pieces he's allowed you to do have always been showstoppers and he hates that. Let's face it, Landon doesn't want an equal. He wants someone to continue worshiping him. And, I'm glad you're finally done with him because you can do so much better. Don't get me wrong, he's amazing at what he does, but it doesn't necessarily make him a good boyfriend."

By the time Patty was done with her tirade, Kaia's mouth was wide open. Little did the other woman know the real reason her and Landon were through, but knowing what she did now, it all made sense. Had her ex really been blocking her opportunities, or had she just been so brainwashed to believe that Bodies in Motion was the best place for her to be? There had been a few opportunities that had come her way and Landon had somehow found fault in them. Come to think of it, he didn't even like her giving the kids lessons at the rec center. He'd said that her talents and time were being wasted there. That was the one thing she wouldn't let him talk her out of.

Had her relationship been a sham this entire time but she was too in love to see it? It was certainly worth thinking about but her wound was still too fresh to be objective about the situation. All Kaia knew was that Landon had broken her heart and there was no coming back from that. Hell, he could have cheated and it wouldn't have hurt as much. To know that she meant so little to him, that he could consider this insane proposition from a man who could very well be a psychopath.

"You may be on to something Patty, but it doesn't change the fact that I loved him. And, now we're through. It hurts like hell."

Patty plopped on the couch next to Kaia and put her arm around her shoulders. "I know, hon, but you're strong, beautiful and talented. I know, whatever happens, you're going to succeed."

"I appreciate your vote of confidence. I suppose I'm going to have to get off your couch at some point."

"Don't get me wrong, you're welcome to stay here as long as you like, I just hate seeing you like this. And, I don't want whatever happened between you and Landon to dictate the rest of your life."

"You're absolutely right and thank you for a place to stay. But, I can't stay here forever. Besides, with the way you stock up on ice cream, I'd gain so much weight; you'd have to roll me out the door."

"Hey, some people love chocolate, I love ice cream. It's gotten me through many hard times and lately, I've needed it."

Kaia raised a brow in surprise. Patty was usually so happy-go-lucky and chipper. Sure, she could be a little too chatty and nosey at times, but her heart was in the right place. "What's been happening with you?"

Patty sighed. "It's just...I don't want to sound like I'm complaining"

"You're not complaining if I ask you what's going on."

"I don't want to burden you with my problems."

Kaia shook her head. "We're friends. You could never burden me. Tell me."

"Well, I've been struggling a little lately. I'll probably have to move out of this apartment and move somewhere smaller, and possibly not as safe."

"Oh, no. I'm sorry to hear that. I didn't realize that."

"I've barely been managing my bills, lately, and my parents have helped me out quite a bit to help because they know dancing for a living is my dream. They've always been super supportive of me. But, my dad was recently laid off and they can't help me anymore. They want to and knowing them, they'd still send me something when they clearly can't afford it. I couldn't take anything from them now when they need it so badly."

"Patty, you should have said something to me."

"I couldn't have done that. It's not like any of us are rich in the company. Most of us are just getting by."

"I have some savings left over from the insurance policy my mother left me. I don't want you to move into an unsafe situation."

"Absolutely not. You may need that money for yourself someday."

Patty had no idea how close she hit the mark. In fact, there was no way she could continue living with Landon and their lease was up next month. Living in close quarters with him would simply be too much for her emotional well-being. An idea popped into her head... "How about having a roommate instead."

"The thought crossed my mind but I'm uncomfortable living with strangers and everyone at the dance troupe has their own things. I...I know people accuse me of being nosey, but I overheard Landon speaking on the phone about money. From what I gather, a large investment in coming this way. He also mentioned something about being to pay more to the dancers. I know that would be a huge help for me and a lot of the others. Miranda has family overseas she sends money to. And, Colin is helping to foot the bill for his grandmother's nursing home care because his parents are having financial struggles. And then, Jackie has a child to take care of. A lot of us could use the extra cash. I hope whoever it was he was talking to comes through. It's not like dancing jobs are easy to come by. It's a competitive field."

Hearing Patty say that put things in perspective for her. Knowing some of her fellow dancers were having financial difficulties, while she was in a position to help, changed things. How could she walk away from Blaise's proposal in all good conscience when so many peoples' livelihoods were in the palm of her hand?

There was still a lot for her to consider now, but, at least, she had a solution for Patty. "How about you and I room together? My lease is up next month and I'm sure we can find something reasonable if we split rent and utilities."

Patty stroked her chin. "I do enjoy having my own space but I if I have to have a roommate, you'd be my best option." She grinned. "Let's do this."

"Cool. When is your lease up?"

"I'm on a month to month, so all I have to do is give a thirty-day notice. But what about Landon?"

That wasn't a name she was interested in hearing right now. "What about him?"

"I mean, wouldn't you be leaving him in a lurch?"

If she only knew. "I think it would be a little awkward living with an ex. I'm still trying to figure out how I'm going to live out the rest of the month the same space with him."

"You can always stay here. I don't mind."

"That's a sweet offer but I should probably use this time to pack. I'll figure out a way to cohabitate with Landon as peacefully as I can."

"You two must have had an awful argument if it's kept you away from dance practice." Patty frowned. "You're not leaving Bodies in Motion, are you?"

Kaia didn't have the answer to that question and it was on the tip of her tongue to say just that when Patty's buzzer rang.

"Hmm, I wonder who that could be." She stood up and walked to her door. "Who is it?"

"Blaise Lundgaard."

Kaia stiffened at the sound of his voice. How had he found her?

Patty turned to her with, bewilderment marring her face. "The guy who's backing the troupe? He's the one who invited us to his penthouse for the get-together, right?"

Kaia could only nod.

"What is he doing here?"

"He came to see me."

Chapter Eight

Luckily for Blaise, someone was walking out of the building as he stood outside. He quickly held the door open and walked in. He moved upstairs of the apartment building the detective had given him. He'd found her location through her cell phone. It was probably unethical to pay someone to access this information but where Kaia was concerned, there were no lengths he'd wouldn't go to.

The surprise on Patty's face when she opened the door might have amused him in other circumstances, but he was a man on a mission.

"Mr. Lundgaard! How did you get through the security door?"

Blaise raised a brow. He was too impatient to answer such an obvious question. Using his considerable height, he looked over Patty's head and his gaze locked on a gaping Kaia.

She wore a pair of leggings and an oversized off-the-shoulder sweatshirt that seemed to swallow her petite frame. Her hair was piled on top of her head in a large afro puff and her face was bare of makeup but she was still gorgeous. Her beautiful brown skin had an ethereal glow to it. Heat coursed through his body and his cock stirred in his excitement at seeing her again.

Her plump lips were slightly parted and he desperately wanted to taste them. Without taking his gaze off of Kaia, he spoke to Patty. "Are you going to invite me in?"

Patty moved aside allowing him entrance. "Please, come in."

"Kaia. Gather your belongings. I've come to take you home."

His words must have activated her because she jumped off the couch. "Take me home? I think not. I'm not going anywhere with you."

So, it appeared she wanted to play this the hard way. A grin curved his lips. "I see." He turned to Patty. "So how are things with your parents, Patty?"

The redhead furrowed her brows, her confusion clear. "Uh...they're doing fine."

"You said you were from Tennessee, correct?"

Patty nodded. "A little town about an hour away from Nashville."

"Oh, yes, I think I remember reading something online recently about a small town in Tennessee that was hit hard by the recession. A few major companies had to lay off several employees. Hopefully, that hasn't affected anyone you know." Blaise watched Patty intently to read her expression.

She blushed, reacting exactly as he predicted she would. "Actually, my father was one of the people who was laid off."

"I'm very sorry to hear that. What did he do?"

"Uh, he was a marketing director. But, he's resilient. Hopefully, he can find something soon."

"I can imagine this is a stressful situation for you. Most dancers barely make enough to get by. Were they helping you out?"

This time, Patty nearly turned as red as her hair. "I...uh, yes. I was just telling Kaia that I'll probably have to move soon but— well, I'm sorry. I don't want to bore you with the details."

"You can't bore me if I asked. Perhaps, I could be of some assistance." He reached into the breast pocket of his jacket and pulled out his platinum business card holder. He took one out and handed it to her. "I happen to have an office building in Memphis. We're expanding in that area and looking for some qualified applicants. I'm almost certain our marketing department is also hiring. Have your father contact my assistant whose information is also on that card and see if we can set up and interview for him."

Patty looked down at the card almost as if she was trying to determine the validity of his offer. "Are you serious?"

"I do not jest when it comes to matters of business or if it's something I really want." He turned his gaze in Kaia's direction to make sure she received the full impact of his statement.

She returned his stare with narrowed eyes and pursed lips. It was okay because he'd have that beautiful mouth moaning his name soon enough.

"Wow, Mr. Lundgaard, I don't know what to say. This is quite generous of you."

"Like I said, there are no guarantees but the least I can do is get him an interview."

"That's more than fair. Thank you. Dad will be thrilled. And this would mean so much to our family. And if I didn't get a chance to thank you before for investing in Bodies in Motion, I'm very appreciative. We all are."

"I'm glad to hear that, Patty. But please, call me Blaise. If you don't mind, can I borrow Miss Benson for a moment, please? I'd like to have a private word with her."

Patty's brows shot up before she looked in Kaia's direction and then back at him. "Uh...sure. You know what, I have to go downstairs to the laundry room and throw a load of clothes in any way. Just give me a second."

Patty disappeared to the back of her apartment for a minute and returned with a basket of clothing. She turned to her temporary roommate and asked, "Do you have anything for me to wash?"

Kaia silently shook her head.

"Okay, I'll be back in a bit."

Once Patty was out of the apartment, Kaia jumped off the couch. "Did you stalk me or something? What the hell are you doing here?"

"Stalking...that's an interesting word. I'd rather call it, accepting a challenge. You threw down the gauntlet when you up and disappeared. It was very short-sighted of you to not think I'd come looking for you."

"You have no idea how crazy you sound right now."

"Not crazy, determined."

"How did you find me anyway?"

"I'm a man of means, which grants me access to certain information that others may not be privy too. Let's leave it at that."

"Well, you've wasted your time coming here because I don't intend on going anywhere with you."

Blaise smirked and placed his hands behind his back. From the moment he'd set eyes on Kaia, he was determined to have her. But one thing he learned through his dealings in business was that in order to achieve any goal, one had to study the objective thoroughly before executing. And, Kaia Benson was a favorite subject of his. The file Blaise had the security agency compile on her told him everything about her, and probably things she didn't know herself. He knew everything from where she'd gone to school since pre-school to what her favorite place to eat was. And, he knew exactly what buttons to push to get her to agree to come with him.

"I see. That's disappointing to hear. I never took you for someone who didn't care about the well-being of her friends. Take Ms. Greer for instance," he said referring to Patty.

Kaia balled her little fists at her sides and she looked as if she wanted to take a swing at him. She really was adorable in her anger. "What about her?" she asked through clenched teeth.

"You're not deaf. You heard the conversation we just had. Her father was just laid off. As I already pointed out, the dancers in Bodies in Motion are barely making enough to get by. I'm quite certain Ms. Greer's parents were supplementing her lifestyle. What do you think will happen to your friend once Bodies in Motion shuts down?"

"So, you're still going to hold that over my head? Wasn't it enough that you're the reason Landon and I broke up? Now, you want to turn me into some kind of sex slave."

Landon threw his head back and laughed, tickled by her righteous indignation. "Has anyone ever told you that you're adorable when you're angry?"

"Fuck you."

"Oh, my dear, I intend to. And, you're going to love every second of it. Getting back to what you previously said; I'm not the cause of your breakup. If Landon loved you as you deserved to be loved, then he would have fought for the relationship tooth and nail. Second, I don't need a sex slave. If all I wanted was sex, there are a number of women I could get it from with a snap of my fingers. Do I make myself clear?"

Kaia crossed her arms over her chest and kept her head down.

"Look at me when I'm talking to you."

She remained defiant in her stance, ignoring his command.

He closed the distance between them and grasped her by the forearms. "Look at me," he said, injecting more steel in his voice.

She raised her head and her eyes glistened with the suspicious sheen of tears. "You knew, didn't you?"

"I knew what?"

"You knew about Patty's father?"

"Yes." He saw no point in denying it. "Just as I know about Ms. Gutierrez sending money to her family in Panama. Or, Mr. Jefferson taking care of the grandmother who raised him. And then, there's Ms. Valentine who's a single mother. That can't be easy for her to support a child on her income. I mean thankfully she has the help of her mother who from my understanding is on disability. I wonder how they'd fair if Bodies in Motion were to go under. I imagine that a monthly check from the government might be hard to stretch for three people. And of course, there's—"

"Okay. Stop. I get it. You had us all investigated."

"I'm a thorough man, especially when it comes to something I want badly enough."

"I just don't understand. Why me? Why can't you just leave me alone?"

"Sometimes, I think showing may be better than telling but especially so in this case." Before she could react, Blaise pulled her against him and lowered his head. The second his lips touched hers, his cock jumped to attention. Her lips were so soft and sweet. They tasted of honey.

Perhaps, it was because she was in shock that Kaia didn't resist right away, she remained still in his arms for a few seconds before trying to turn her head away from his. He grasped her chin between his fingers while keeping one arm hooked around his waist.

He crushed her mouth beneath his again, wanting more of this. He needed to taste the warm recesses of her mouth, needed it. "Open up for me, *kæreste*."

When she refused, he grabbed her hair and gave it a yank, making her gasp. Taking advantage of her parted lips, his slipped his tongue into her mouth and took what he sought.

Kaia pushed against his chest but Blaise refused to budge. He hungered for this woman like a man who hadn't eaten in days. He needed her like oxygen and this kiss was hardly enough. Without breaking the tight seal of his lips over hers, he lifted Kaia off her feet and carried her the short distance to the couch. He lay her down and immediately fell on top of her, claiming her lips once more.

Everything about her was driving him insane with need, from the little whimpers in the back of her throat to her scent. He wanted to rip her clothes off and fuck her right here and now but he realized that they didn't have much time before Patty returned. So, he'd settle for a little taste. He moved his hands down the center of her body until he reached the juncture between her legs.

She managed to twist her head away from his. "No, don't."

"I must," he muttered burying his face against her neck and nipping her tender flesh. She felt so warm beneath her palm.

Unable to help himself, he slipped his hand in her leggings and into her panties. He felt the moisture of her pussy and the heat was beckoning him to explore further. Blaise slid his finger along her slit before dipping it inside her slick folds.

"Stop," she gasped. The word sounded weak and unconvincing.

"Your mouth says, no but your body says yes. You're so wet and slick for me. It's okay that you want me, Kaia, because I want you, too, and I'm going to make you feel so good." He moved his finger in and out of her, coating his finger with her juices.

He lifted his head to meet her gaze. There were so many expressions in her eyes; confusion, anger and...lust. It was that last emotion that he would focus on. Slowly, he eased his finger out of her and brought it to his mouth. Blaise never broke eye contact as he sucked it into his mouth.

"Delicious."

Reluctantly, he pulled away from her and rolled off the couch. Now that he'd had a taste of her, Blaise knew that he wouldn't rest until he had all of her. But he'd give her the time she needed, especially now that he knew she wasn't as averse to his touch as she claimed.

Blaise stood up and adjusted his clothing. "Get your belongings. We're leaving."

Kaia sat up, her body trembling. "I don't want to go anywhere with you."

"That's too bad because you know exactly what will happen if you don't. Not only will I withdraw the funding for Bodies in Motions, I'll make sure that every single one of the dancers never work in this industry again."

Kaia jumped to her feet. "You can't do that!"

He raised a brow. "You don't think so? I'm a very wealthy man with an extensive network of connections. I suggest you don't challenge me."

Chapter Nine

Tears glided down her cheeks as she looked absently out the window of the car. She'd already figured that Blaise Lundgaard was a monster but she didn't know how frightening he could be. That he would threaten her friends simply because he couldn't get what he wanted was beyond reason. She hated his guts and wanted nothing to do with this so-called deal of his, but how could she say no when he had the power to destroy so many lives.

When Patty returned from the laundry room, Kaia had already gathered her belongings. She gave a brief explanation to her friend that Blaise was taking her back home and she'd call later. Thankfully Patty didn't bombard her with a slew of questions, probably because she was just as confused about the situation as Kaia was.

"Are you going to sulk for the remainder of the ride?" Blaise placed his hand on her shoulder.

She flinched away from his touch. It wasn't because she hated it. She pulled away because she didn't. Kaia was still trying to figure out what had come over her in Patty's apartment. Though she despised this man, it baffled her how she'd responded to him touching her so intimately. She'd only had two lovers in her life. Her first was a clumsy encounter during her freshman year when she'd hooked up with a guy she'd met at a party. To her secret shame, she couldn't remember his name. After that incident, she realized that one-night stands weren't for her. Though she didn't regret losing her virginity, she did have remorse about not being emotionally connected to the person she lost it to.

With Landon, it had been special, or so she thought. But Blaise... he was on a whole other level and she wasn't quite sure what to make of it.

"You can't keep ignoring me," Blaise spoke again, breaking into her thoughts.

"You forced me to come, you didn't say I had to converse with you."

"It would make things a lot less tense if you drop this ice princess act."

She whirled around in her seat, her anger renewed. "Are you serious?

After what you've done, did you think I'd be all smiles and sunshine? You are crazy. What is it with you? Why couldn't you leave me be? I was happy before you came crashing into my life. I loved what I did and I was in a relationship. My life was just fine before you came along."

"Was it? I did, after all, expose you to the kind of man you were cohabitating with."

Even though Landon didn't deserve it, she felt compelled to defend him. "Only because you put a tremendous amount of pressure on his shoulders. You made other backers pull out just so you could make the dance company vulnerable financially. You threw this insane proposition in my face and you had all the dancers investigated. What kind of man are you?"

"A thorough man. I admit I was a bit heavy handed with Bodies in Motion. However, don't you think it was to my benefit to know what type of company I was investing in and the type of people who worked for it? Doing an investigation is standard business practice, my dear. But let's cut to the chase. You're really upset right now because you've discovered that you're not as adverse to my touch as you assumed you'd be. In fact, you liked it a lot."

Unable to hold his gaze, she looked away. "You must have imagined that."

Blaise chuckled. It was an infuriating sound that taunted her. "So, it was my imagination when I slid my finger into your juicy cunt and it practically soaked my hand. Your muscles tightened around my finger. You wanted it so bad, you couldn't stop purring. You can pretend that you didn't want me, but your body says otherwise. In fact, I think you may need another demonstration."

Blaise reached for her but Kaia slid as far away from him as possible. She shook her head vehemently. "Don't." She gestured to the driver, who even though he was staring straight ahead, could see and possibly hear everything. She didn't want a witness to her shame.

Blaise briefly spared a glance at the driver before hitting the button to make the partition go up, giving them privacy. "Problem solved."

This time when he reached out for her, there was no avoiding him. He pulled her into his arms. As Kaia learned earlier, he was simply too strong to fight off, but perhaps if she remained unresponsive, he'd get the hint.

To her surprise, Blaise didn't kiss her lips. Instead, he leaned forward and pulled her earlobe between his lips and began to nibble. He kissed and licked the shell of her ear before dragging his tongue down the side of her neck leaving a wet trail. The sensual stroke of his tongue created a tingling sensation that started in her core and slowly spread throughout her body.

Kaia tried her hardest to resist the heat building within her but when he cupped one of her breasts, she released a soft moan. Blaise moved his hand beneath her shirt and pushed her bra up, exposing her bare breasts to his touch. Her nipple puckered beneath the pad of his thumb and she put her hands on his shoulders with the intention of pushing him away, but instead, she found herself clinging to him.

Before she realized what was happening, Kaia found herself flat on her back with Blaise on top of her. He raised her top baring her to his hungry gaze. She attempted to cross her arms over her chest but Blaise stopped her, capturing both wrists in one large hand. "Never hide yourself from me," he practically barked the words, sending a shiver of fear and excitement through her at the same time.

What was wrong with her? Why wasn't she fighting to free herself? The way he stared at her body was like a hungry lion eyeing a particularly succulent cut of meat.

"You're so beautiful. I can't wait to have all of you." Her tweaked one nipple between his thumb and forefinger. An involuntary moan escaped her lips and Kaia arched her back.

He lowered his head, took one taut tip in his mouth and suckled gently at first and then more voraciously.

"Oh, God," she moaned, wiggling beneath the erotic ministration of his mouth.

He sucked on her nipple for what seemed like a very long time because she could feel her body hurtling toward its peak. Just as she thought she'd fall apart, Blaise lifted his head and released her. He sat up and adjusted her clothing. "You see, my dear, you're not so adverse to my touch."

He didn't seem nearly as affected as she was. Embarrassed, Kaia sat up and fixed her clothing. "This is all just a game to you, isn't it?"

"This is no game, my dear."

"You just did that to prove a point."

"No. I did it because you're mine." He gripped her hand and placed it on his lap. She came in contact with what felt like a considerable erection. "You see, *kæreste*, this is what you do to me. I can barely control myself around you. You said that you wouldn't enjoy being with me, I just wanted to show you otherwise. But, we'll discuss that later. We're here."

Kaia noticed for the first time that the car had stopped in front of his building. He hit the button on the partition and once down, nodded to his driver. The chauffeur opened Blaise's door and Blaise, in turn, opened hers. He gently took her by the arm and led her up to his penthouse. Though she tried to pull away from him, Blaise wouldn't allow it. His grip tightened on her arm.

"You don't have to hold me so tight."

"I'm just making sure you don't get away from me this time."

"I have a feeling that no matter where I go, you'd find me."

A smile curved his lips, giving him a devilish appearance. "You finally seem to be getting the idea."

And, that's the part that scared her the most.

Once they were inside his penthouse, Kaia looked around. "Where's Aneka?"

"She's probably in the study with her tutor. I take her education very seriously."

"Oh."

"Have a seat while I take your things to your room."

"I'm not sharing a room with you."

"Relax. I'm not completely insensitive to the situation. You'll be set up in the spare bedroom until further notice."

"So, this is happening?" she said more to herself than to him.

"Was there any doubt?"

Blaise took her overnight bag and headed up the stairs. She restrained the childish impulse to yell out that she hoped he'd trip.

With a heavy sigh, she took a seat on the couch and dropped her head in the palms of her hands. What had she gotten herself into and how would she get through this ordeal? If she backed out, Kaia was almost certain he'd follow through on his promise of ruining the lives of her friends.

And even if he didn't, it wouldn't stop his pursuit of her. There seemed to be only one way she could get out of this without completely breaking apart, and that was doing things on her own terms.

She was so deep in thought she didn't hear anyone enter the room.

"Kaia! *Jeg er så glad, du er her*!"

Obsessed

She raised her head to see Aneka wheeling toward her. She pasted a smile on her face. The last thing she wanted was for the child to know how upsetting being here was. It wasn't Aneka's fault that her brother was a brute. "Hi, Aneka. I hope that means you're happy to see me because I didn't understand a word you said."

The young blonde smacked herself on the forehead and laughed. "I'm sorry. I sometimes forget to switch languages, but I said, I'm happy that you're here. Did you come to visit me?"

"Well...actually..." she wasn't exactly sure how to answer that. How could she tell this sweet child that she was only here because her brother had blackmailed her?

"Kaia is actually going to stay with us for a little while," Blaise said as he walked into the room.

Aneka gasped. *Er det sandt?* I mean, are you serious?"

Kaia looked at Blaise and then back at Aneka. There was no backing down now. "I, uh, guess so."

"Oh, that's wonderful news! We will have so much fun together." Aneka looked up at her brother. "Does this mean you'll get rid of my nurse and Kaia can be my fulltime companion?"

"Kaia has other obligations, precious, but she'll certainly be spending more time here. Why aren't you with your tutor?"

"He's grading my test, so I'm taking a break. I thought I heard you speaking with someone out here. Kaia, I was so disappointed when you left the other day because you said you'd come back to my room. But, you never did. I thought you didn't want to be my friend anymore."

Kaia felt like a jerk knowing that she'd hurt Aneka's feelings. It wasn't as if she could tell this child that she'd skipped out on dinner because her boyfriend was a louse. And that Blaise was an even bigger one.

"I'm sorry you felt that I didn't want to be friends with you, sweetheart. I wasn't feeling well, and I didn't want to make you sick."

A smile settled on Aneka's face. "I'm glad to hear that, not that you were sick but that Blaise was telling the truth."

Kaia's brows shot up and she turned to Blaise.

He shrugged. "Aneka didn't believe me when I told her that you were sick. For some reason, she believed that I was making it up to spare her feelings."

Aneka shrugged. "Well, it wouldn't have been the first time you tried to protect my feelings. Kaia, Blaise is a good big brother but sometimes he can be a bit overbearing. I had a group of friends...or at least, I believed they were my friends but they only wanted to play with me because of all the expensive toys I had. Blaise had overheard them saying this and told them to leave and never return. He, then, told me that they had family emergencies. But, I had overheard them, too. I pretended like I hadn't but..." she shrugged.

Kaia's heart went out to the girl. That was quite a burden for a twelve-year-old to carry. "Well, you're better off without them. But, I'm your friend. And, I like you because you're sweet, kind and smart. Anyone who can't see that, well, that's their problem."

Aneka smiled. "I know that. I'm awesome."

The girl's response took her by surprise, making Kaia laugh. "That's the spirit."

Just then, a young man with dark hair stepped in the room. "Aneka, I've finished grading your test. You missed one but we can go over it until you get the hang of it." The man nodded his head in Blaise's direction. "Good afternoon, Mr. Lundgaard."

"Alex. I trust my sister's studies are going well?"

"She's doing amazing. She has a strong aptitude for math. She's already at a high school level. I'm going to introduce some college material if she continues to excel."

Blaise nodded seeming satisfied. "Good. Be sure to leave her daily progress report on my desk."

"Of course. Come along, Aneka."

Aneka turned to Kaia. "You'll be here when I've finished my lessons for the day?"

"Sure."

"Great. There's something in my room I'd like to show you." She smiled before wheeling herself toward her tutor.

Once the two of them left, Blaise sighed. "She puts on a brave face most of the time, sometimes she is sensitive about her condition and how other people act around her. I appreciate that you don't treat her as if she's delicate or that she's a bother."

"Why would I do that? She's a sweet girl."

"You'd be surprised. Some people don't realize how patronizing they can be toward someone with special needs. Most of the time, I know they don't mean it but my sister always picks up on it."

Kaia nodded. "I can imagine."

Silence fell between the two of them as Kaia tried to figure out what she needed to say. Blaise stared at her with his intense blue gaze making her squirm in her seat. "Please don't do that."

"Do what?"

"Look at me like that."

"How?"

"Like you want to do things to me."

"You have no idea."

Kaia took a deep breath. It was now or never. "Look Blaise…you have me backed in a corner. And the way I see it, I don't have much of a choice but to agree to this crazy scheme of yours."

"You make it seem as if you're being sentenced to time in prison. This could be mutually beneficial for us both, Kaia. As I've already demonstrated, we're sexually compatible."

"This isn't just about sex, Blaise. I have terms of my own if you want me to agree to this."

He shrugged. "I wouldn't expect anything less. Let's go to my office and discuss this."

Chapter Ten

Blaise stared at the contract his lawyer had faxed back to him. Kaia had insisted on a written agreement. Her first demand came as no surprise. She wanted him to okay the funding of Bodies in Motion so that he could no longer dangle that carrot over her head. Her next request was that he saw to the needs of her friends in the dance company. The only thing she requested for herself was that she continue to dance without any interference on his behalf.

He had almost expected her to ask for something extravagant for herself but she didn't. It only spoke to her character. Her last demand, however, was a bone of contention for him. She had the option to walk away after Aneka had her surgery.

Aneka's first consultation was coming up and Blaise was told that the surgery could be scheduled within a few months. Though he'd reluctantly agreed, he had no intention of letting her go. He was certain he could figure a way to keep her from leaving but until then, he would give her several reasons to make her want to stay.

Perhaps, he was being underhanded but a woman like Kaia Benson only came along once in a lifetime and he didn't intend to allow this opportunity to slip through his fingers.

Was it love? Blaise couldn't answer that question for sure, but he knew that she was his first waking thought and throughout the day he could barely get any work done because he was consumed with images of her. He'd imagined what it would be like when he finally made love to her.

His dick got hard as he thought about sliding into her tight pussy and becoming one with her. She was reluctant now, but he would make sure when he finally took her that she'd love every second of it.

Maybe he was crazy in aggressive he was in his pursuit of her but he simply couldn't help himself. He wasn't the way he was because he'd had a fucked-up childhood, in fact, growing up he had a pretty average home life, better than most in fact. Some would say he'd lived a sheltered life but after his parents were killed in the same car crash that crippled Aneka, something inside him hardened. He realized the world wasn't as nice and idyllic as he had believed. It hardened him, made him cynical, especially when it came to women.

But Kaia was like a breath of fresh air in his polluted world, and he intended to do whatever it took to keep him at her side always. This contract was just a stepping stone.

He ran his fingers over her signature which had been freshly signed this morning. "You're mine now, Miss Benson. Now and forever," he whispered to himself.

Just as he placed the contract in his desk drawer, his phone rang. The red flashing light indicated the call was coming from his assistant. "Yes, Edith."

"You have a visitor in the lobby who's quite insistent on seeing you."

He raised a brow wondering who could be visiting him at his New York office. He had no meetings lined up today. "Who is it?"

"A Ms. Sorensen is here to see you."

The mention of Lisbeth's name caused his frown to deepen. He hadn't seen her since he and Aneka had left Denmark. He and Lisbeth did not exactly part on friendly terms. She'd accused him of wasting her time when he'd politely informed her that he no longer wished to date her.

What was she doing in the states? Though he was tempted to send her away, his curiosity got the better of him. Besides, his company did a fair amount of business with her father's, so it wouldn't hurt to see what she wanted.

"Send her in."

Moments later, Edith opened his office door only for Lisbeth to breeze past her without waiting for her to move out of the way.

"Really, Blaise, was it necessary to keep me waiting so long. Back home I was allowed to go to your office without any trouble. The security guards downstairs were very rude. But, what do you expect from Americans?" She flipped her coiffed locks over her shoulder dramatically.

"Will that be all, Mr. Lundgaard?" Edith asked from the door.

Lisbeth turned around to wave her hand dismissively. "That will be all, Edna."

Edith firmed her lips but remained where she stood.

"Thank you, Edith. I'll call you if I need anything else."

His assistant shook Lisbeth a narrow-eyed stare before closing the door.

"Such insolence," Lisbeth muttered as she shrugged out of her jacket to reveal a sheer blouse that showed off a black bra beneath and a pair of assets that made Blaise do a double take. It was clear that his former lover had had some recent surgical enhancements. While Lisbeth presented the perfect picture of Nordic Blonde beauty, he couldn't help but compare her to Kaia. Where Lisbeth was fair, Kaia's skin was like dark silk. Lisbeth was tall and statuesque and with her newly altered body, her curves were more pronounced. But, Kaia was compact and petite and molded from sheer perfection.

Seeing his old lover left him cold.

"What are you doing in New York, Lisbeth?"

"Father is here on business and he asked me to come along with him to play hostess. My mother hates transatlantic trips."

It was more than likely that Peter Sorensen had left his wife home so he could spend time with his mistress who wasn't much older than Lisbeth. "I see. And, why are you here exactly?"

She raised a brow. "I heard you and you dear sister were in New York for a few months and I just had to come by and see you. How is that sweet child by the way?"

Obsessed

"Aneka is fine. But, I'm still curious to know why you bothered to stop by; considering the last time we spoke, you said I'd wasted your time. As far as I'm concerned, that was the end of our association."

She pouted and leaned forward in an obvious ploy to show off her breasts. "You can't hold that against me. Of course, I was upset that you would end things after I thought things were going well between us. Besides, I don't see why we can't be friends. Anyway, my father is having a little gathering tonight and I'd really like it if you can come."

Tonight, he was looking forward to spending time with Kaia, but it wouldn't hurt if he brought her along so she could get a taste of what it would be like to be with him. From time to time, she would have to mingle with his business associates and their significant others. Now that he thought about it, it didn't seem like a bad idea. Besides, it would give him the opportunity to see Kaia dressed up.

"Leave the details with Edith and me and my date will be there."

Lisbeth's mouth formed an 'o', giving her the appearance of a fish on a hook. "A date? You're seeing someone else?"

"Obviously, if I'm dating her then that usually means yes. Now, if there isn't anything else you wanted, I've got a lot of work to do."

"Who is she? Do I know her? Is she an American? I mean, it can't be that serious. You haven't been in this country that long."

Blaise leaned forward, steepling his fingers together. "Do I take this to mean, my invitation has been rescinded...*friend*?"

Angry splotches of red colored her cheeks. "Of course not. It's just a surprise is all. I mean, I didn't expect you to end up with someone else so soon after we broke things off."

"Well, it's a good thing that I'm not interested in what you think. Anyway, as I already stated, I have a lot of work to do."

Lisbeth pursed her lips and grabbed her jacket. "Fine, I suppose, I'll see you and your little date tonight then."

Blaise inclined his head forward in acknowledgment. He realized she was still fishing and he wasn't interested in taking the bait. He turned his attention back to his computer hoping she'd get the hint.

He was met with a frustrated sigh as the sound of her heels stomped on the floor. She slammed the door behind her.

Tonight was going to be interesting indeed.

Kaia was nervous when she stepped into the studio for the first time in a few days. She hadn't seen Landon since she'd stormed out of their apartment and the only dancer she'd had any contact within the company had been Patty, who had left her several messages since Blaise had come to pick her up.

She didn't want to think about Blaise and that stupid contract he'd had drawn up. She wasn't sure how he'd managed to get something drawn up so quickly but after she'd told him of her demands, he got on the phone with his lawyers.

When she'd come downstairs that morning, a contract was ready for her to sign. She felt as if she had signed her life away. Afterwards, Blaise's driver, Roger, took Kaia to her old apartment where she packed up her clothing and dance gear. Thankfully, Landon was already gone. Once she was done, Roger dropped Kaia off in front of the dance studio.

At least, she still had dance. It had been one of her conditions... that she be able to continue working with the dance troupe and volunteering at the rec center. Though her and Landon were no longer together, she, at least, still had Bodies in Motion and she wouldn't allow anyone to get in the way of what she loved doing.

As she looked around the studio, most of the dancers were already there. Landon stood off to the corner helping Deena with her stretches. The way they stood together made it appear as if there was something going on between them. Her heart briefly felt as if it was being squeezed in her chest as she looked at the intimate picture the two of them created. It had been no secret among the dancers that Deena had a thing for Landon. It had never bothered Kaia before because she'd been secure in her relationship. But now that she knew what she did about Landon, Kaia couldn't help but wonder if anything ever happened between them while she and Landon were still together.

Patty was the first one to notice her. She ran over to her. "Kaia! You're here!" She pulled Kaia into a tight embrace. "I was worried about you when you left in a hurry with..." The redhead stopped and looked around. By now, the other dancers had noticed her arrival and gathered around her.

"Where the hell have you been?" Colin demanded. "We were all worried about you, and Landon's been tight-lipped."

"Oh, I just had to take a few days to myself to sort out some personal issues." It's not like she wanted to shout out at the top of her lungs that her rat bastard ex had basically sold her off to keep the company running.

"Well, it's good to have you back." Miranda tapped her on the shoulder.

A few of the other dancers welcomed her back. By now, a red-faced Landon joined the group with a sullen Deena. In fact, Deena raised her chin and said, "I'm going to be taking the lead on the swan dance since you can't be bothered to show up to practice."

The swan dance was the centerpiece of the performance, Kaia had helped Landon choreograph the piece. "Is that so?"

"Yeah, it is. You tell her, Landon," Deena looked at Landon expectantly.

If Kaia thought he was red before, his hue now could rival that of a tomato. "Well, if Kaia's back, I think it's best if she takes it. I mean, I wasn't expecting her to return anytime soon." He refused to look the brunette in the eye.

Had he always been this much of a coward? Someone who couldn't stick to his convictions. Why hadn't she seen this before?

"But, you told me last night that it was mine!" Deena practically screamed.

Kaia raised a brow. "Last night?"

Deena glared at her. "That's right. You think you're such hot shit, but you're not the only one with talent around here. We all work our asses off but it's Kaia this and Kaia that. You're not so special, or else Landon wouldn't have been with me last night."

The studio went silent as if everyone was watching a salacious reality show program. Kaia's mouth fell open as she looked at Landon, who refused to meet her gaze. It had only been a few days but he'd already hooked up with Deena?

Maybe, Blaise had done her a favor by exposing Landon for the worm he was. But one thing she wasn't about to do, was getting into a screaming match with Deena, who was clearly unhinged. Deena had never been very friendly toward any of the other dancers and for the most part, she just ignored Kaia unless necessary. But apparently, she'd been harboring a lot of pent-up resentment judging from this outburst.

"Okay, Deena. You want it so badly, how about we compete for it? You perform the piece and then I'll do it. We'll put it to a vote and may the better dancer win."

"You know that wouldn't be fair. Everyone kisses your ass because you're dating Landon."

Obviously, neither Landon nor Patty had told anyone. Kaia laughed. "Landon and I aren't together anymore, so I say you have a pretty fair shot."

A few of the other dancers gasped. Someone said, "Whaaaat?"

Deena seemed to be just as surprised by the news as everyone else. "Well, it doesn't matter because the part belongs to me."

"I think Kaia had a good idea. You two should dance to see who is better for the part," Landon spoke up.

"This is bullshit!" Deena crossed her arms.

"If you think you're the best person for this spot, then I don't see what the problem is," Colin interjected.

"No one asked you, Colin. Fine. I'll do it, but I want Kaia to go first."

Patty leaned over to whisper. "Don't worry, I know you'll kill it. She's just upset because she knows you're the better dancer."

Kaia was coming into this cold. She hadn't had time to stretch or warm up properly. Perhaps that's what

Deena was counting on, but it didn't matter. Kaia stayed ready.

"Fine, I'll go first." She slid out of her leggings and took her shoes off. Kaia did a quick stretch on the bar, before moving to the center of the floor. "I'm ready."

Once the music began to play, she became lost in the rhythm. They'd been working on this piece for several weeks so she knew it like the back of her hand. She could feel herself becoming one with the music. She *was* the music. She jumped high, twirled and kicked. It didn't matter that she wasn't on stage in a theater full of people. She still gave it her all, as she did with everything. When she was finished, she did a split leap, landed on one foot and went into an arabesque, ending the routine.

The room broke out into applause. Kaia knew she killed it. She'd felt it. She hadn't danced in a few days and she missed it. It was simply a part of her.

"Wow, that was pretty amazing," Patty sighed.

"Thanks."

"Well, it looks like everyone has already decided." Deena pouted as she moved to the center of the room.

Once the music started for Deena, she began to do the same routine but Kaia noticed she'd missed several steps. There was no doubt that Deena was talented, everyone in Bodies in Motion was an outstanding dancer, but it was clear that she hadn't mastered this piece. There seemed to be an unexplainable disconnect. Perhaps with more practice, she would have it down.

When Deena's turn was complete, everyone clapped politely but it was nowhere near the exuberance Kaia had received.

"Well, I think, we have a clear winner. Kaia will have the part. Deena, you'll do the dove dance."

"This is bullshit. I should have the part because at least I show up. We don't all get to take personal days. Fuck this," Deena stormed off.

"Just ignore her. She's always throwing a tantrum," Patty assured Kaia.

"I'm not worried out her. She'll get over it."

Landon walked over to them and cleared his throat. "Excuse me, ladies. I was wondering if I could speak privately with Kaia, please."

Kaia rolled her eyes. "Do we have to do this now?"

"I think so. Please, just a few minutes."

She sighed. "Fine." Kaia followed Landon to his office and he closed the door.

"Have a seat," he gestured to the chair in front of the desk.

"No thank you. I'd rather stand."

"Okay," he sat on the edge of his desk and folded his hands in his lap. "I was worried about you when you left in the middle of the night like you did. Why didn't you return my calls?"

"Because I didn't want to talk to you."

"Where did you go?"

"That's none of your business. We're no longer together, so you don't have the right to question my comings and goings."

He raked his fingers through his hair in obvious frustration. "Look, I'm sorry okay. I fucked up. After you left, I realized how you must have felt. I was so focused on saving the company, I didn't take your feelings into consideration."

"Gee, how big of you. Landon, if you just brought me in here to apologize, forget about it. I just want to do my job and that's it."

"That's it? Just like that?"

"What do you want me to say? You're the one who made the decision to give me away without consulting me first. You let me know how little I meant to you, all without saying a word. I sat there, waiting for you to tell Blaise Lundgaard to go to hell, but you couldn't accept his deal fast enough. So yeah, it's like that. Not to mention, you were getting mighty cozy to Deena. Apparently, last night must have been pretty special."

"It wasn't like that. We both stayed late at the studio working on the number."

"Is that what you call it? It seems to me, she thought there was much more to it."

"I have no control over what she believes. And the only reason I told her she could have that part in the show, was because I wasn't sure if you were coming back and you wouldn't return my calls. I was wondering…is there no way we can work this out?"

"Work what out? As far as I'm concerned, you're just my boss."

"It doesn't have to be like that. Are you really ready to throw three years down the drain?"

Kaia was certain she hadn't heard him correctly, but just in case, she had to ask, "Are you high?"

"What?"

"Are. You. High? You're asking me that, after what you did? Even if I were stupid enough to want to work things out with you, I couldn't because of that little deal I've basically been forced into."

"So, you did it?"

"I had no choice." There was already so much at stake, she saw no point in telling him that Blaise had had the rest of the dancers investigated.

Landon snorted. "So, I guess being with a rich man suddenly became an attractive option to you."

Obsessed

Kaia quickly closed the distance between them and smacked him across the face as hard as she could, sending his head to the side. "Are you fucking serious?! You have no idea what it was like to know that I meant so little to you; that I basically had to compromise everything I believe in to save this company. And I wasn't going to mention this before, but he threatened everyone's livelihoods. No one would have been able to find work if Bodies in Motion went under if I hadn't agreed to do this. I'm the only one who gets nothing out of this, so fuck you!"

Kaia turned to leave but Landon grabbed her arm and turned her around and pulled her into his arms. "Kaia, don't leave, I'm sorry I didn't mean to say that. I was just jealous."

Kaia thought she was all out of tears but apparently, she was wrong. She started to cry as Landon tightened his arms around her. She was too upset to push him away even though he was the current cause of her upset. She wished they'd never gone to Denmark and that Blaise had never seen them. Maybe she and Landon would have eventually broken up, but it wouldn't have been like this.

She clung to him as her heart continued to break.

Landon kissed her forehead and whispered. "I'm sorry, Kaia." He rested his chin on her forehead as he continued to hold her.

Just then, the office door flew open. "What the fuck is going on in here?" An angry Blaise stood in the doorway.

Eve Vaughn

Chapter Eleven

After his last meeting, Blaise decided to see Kaia at the dance studio. He was aware that she'd gone to her old apartment to collect her belongings. Blaise was uneasy about Kaia working in such close proximity to Campion, after all, they were freshly broken up. If he had his way, he would have seen to it that Kaia leave Bodies in Motion. He would have bought Kaia her own studio if it meant keeping her away from her ex, but this was what she wanted.

When he made it to the dance studio where Bodies in Motion held their rehearsals, he saw neither Kaia nor Campion were with the rest of the dancers. When Blaise went out in the hallway, he noticed a sullen brunette, slouched against the wall. "Where is Mr. Campion?"

The brunette perked up when she noticed who was speaking to her. "Mr. Lundgaard? It's a pleasure to see you again. I never got the opportunity to thank you for inviting me into your lovely home."

"You're welcome...Miss—"

She flipped her hair over her shoulder and smiled. "You can just call me, Deena. I'm one of the principal dancers in Bodies in Motion."

Blaise was even less interested in talking to Deena than he had been with Lisbeth earlier. "Congratulations. Where may I find Mr. Campion?"

"He's probably in his office with Kaia," she shrugged. "Will there be any more parties at your place? I'd love to visit again."

"I'm sure you would," he murmured as he turned away from her and strode toward the office.

He heard voices coming from behind the door and he hoped it wasn't what he thought was going on. Blaise practically pulled the door from its hinges as he opened it, only to find Kaia in Campion's arms.

The two of them jumped away from each other.

"Mr. Lundgaard," Campion stepped forward with his hand outstretched.

Blaise looked at it pointedly, until the other man dropped his hand. "Give me one good reason, why I don't rip your head off right now."

Campion took a step back. "Mr. Lundgaard, this isn't what it looks like. Kaia was just upset and I was comforting her."

Blaise looked at Kaia. He noticed for the first time that her eyes were puffy and red as if she'd been crying.

"Kaia, get your stuff. We're leaving."

She shook her head and for the first time she spoke since he entered the room. "We're not finished rehearsal. I'm not going anywhere until I'm finished."

He walked over to Kaia and took her by the wrist before pulling her toward the door.

"Stop. This isn't part of our agreement."

"Fuck the agreement," he roared, allowing his jealousy to get the better of him. He didn't care why she'd been in Campion's arms. It was the fact that she'd been there at all, which is what pissed him off.

"Now, wait a minute. You don't have to manhandle her like that."

"Stay out of this, Campion," Blaise roared pulling Kaia along with him.

Kaia continued to fight him as he pulled her outside. He ignored the curious stares from the other dancers. His only concern was getting Kaia as far away from here as possible.

Roger was waiting outside for them on the curb.

"Get in the car, Kaia."

"I'm not going anywhere with you. You are insane!"

Running out of patience, he lifted her off the ground, opened the car door and stuffed her inside.

"I left my stuff in there, you brute!" she yelled.

"Roger, would you mind going inside to collect Ms. Benson's belongings?"

"Yes, sir." The driver nodded and left the vehicle.

"What were you doing in the office with Campion?"

"Making wild passionate love. What the hell did it look like to you? Clearly, I was upset about something and just as he said, he was comforting me, even though he was the one who pissed me off in the first place. Do you have any idea how you just made me look in there? What will my colleagues think, seeing you drag me out of the studio like some bratty child?"

"I don't give a shit about what any of them think. You're the one who wanted to sign an agreement and I fulfilled my end. The dance company gets its money, I leave your friends alone and you continue to dance. But I made it explicitly clear that you have no further contact with Campion that is not explicitly related to dance. But, what do I fucking find? You're in his arms. I wonder what would have happened next if I had arrived a few minutes later?"

"And, if you would have arrived a few minutes sooner, you would have seen me slapping the shit out of him. Is this how it's going to be for the rest of my time with you? You acting like a jealous idiot when I so much as talk to someone else?"

Blaise didn't answer that question right away because he wasn't sure if he had an answer she wanted to hear. "You belong to me, Kaia. And no one will touch you, but me."

"You said, you'd give me time."

Blaise shrugged. "Did I?"

"You said, you wouldn't do anything that I didn't want."

"Oh, but what I plan on doing to you, you're very much going to want it."

Kaia looked as if she wanted to say something but Roger returned with her bag. "I will fight you tooth and nail."

Despite how tense the moment was, Blaise couldn't help but chuckle. He admired her spirit. Even in her fury, she turned him on.

Kaia turned in her seat and stared out the window silently as they headed back to his penthouse.

"Relax, Kaia. Do you really think being my woman will be such an ordeal? I could grant all of your wildest wishes. Name it and it's yours."

She turned to him a raised brow. "Really? Anything I want."

"Yes."

"I want my freedom."

He tightened his lips. "Anything except that."

"Then, there's nothing else I want from you."

With the gauntlet thrown down, Blaise was more than ready to accept that challenge. After tonight, Kaia would be his in every sense of the word. And, there was nothing she could do about it.

Kaia would have gone straight to her room once they returned to the penthouse but Aneka was in the living room with her nurse. The adolescent was looking at something on her tablet while her nurse was leafing through a magazine.

As soon as Kaia and Blaise walked into the room, she lifted her head and grinned from ear to ear. Kaia swore that if it wasn't for this little girl, she would have driven a stake through Blaise's heart by now.

"Kaia, come! You have to see this video I was watching online. It's your dance troupe when you were in Copenhagen. Someone must have filmed it." Aneka waved her over.

Kaia sat on the sofa, closest to Aneka's chair. Sure enough, there was a video of the performance. It was called sunset. Everyone else had been wearing light unitards but she wore red because she was the setting sun. Landon had been the moonlight.

They had all poured their hearts and souls into the piece. She remembered how excited everyone had been when Landon had put together the European tour. The night before the performance in Denmark, Kaia must have eaten some bad fish because she'd been throwing up, but she didn't want to miss the performance. Even though she still wasn't 100%, she'd given her all at that festival.

Those were happier times.

"Are you okay, Kaia?" Aneka frowned, her blue eyes so much like her brother's brimming with concern.

"Yes, why do you ask?"

"Because you're crying?"

Sure enough, tears slid unheeded down her cheeks. Kaia quickly wiped them away. "I'm sorry. It must make me happy to see that. I'd never been to Europe before that tour and I just remember having a good time."

"Oh," the child relaxed and smiled. "You were my favorite part of the festival. I wanted to meet you that day, but you had already left when Blaise and I went backstage to meet you."

"Well, it looks like everything has worked out. If you don't mind, I think I need to go upstairs and rest."

"Oh, okay. I had a question for you."

"What's that?"

"Well, if it's okay with Blaise, I was wondering if I could come watch one of your rehearsals. I'm sure we could work around Alex's schedule."

With how tense things were at the company right now, Kaia wasn't sure that it was the best place for her to be. Besides, after Blaise had made an ass of himself today, Kaia wasn't sure if she was still welcome. "I suppose it would be okay if your brother says it is."

"Oh, Blaise won't mind. Will you Blaise?" Aneka turned to her brother, who had been watching them quietly from the other side of the room.

"We'll see, precious. In the meantime, Kaia and I have a few things to discuss."

"Sure." The girl returned her attention to her tablet.

Kaia headed upstairs with Blaise on her heels. When she entered her room, she saw two boxes on her bed; one long rectangular one and a smaller one that looked like a shoebox.

"What is this?" She turned to Blaise who'd followed Kaia into her room.

"I came by the studio earlier because I wanted to let you know that I've been invited to a get-together tonight with some business associates, and I needed you to accompany me. I gave my assistant your measurements and had her order something appropriate for you."

She shuddered. "I'm not even going to ask how you know my measurements."

A smile twisted his lips. "While I'm sure your imagination is running wild with debauchery, I simply looked at the labels of the clothing you have hanging in the closet."

"Oh." Even though she didn't like the idea of him rifling through her stuff, she supposed it wasn't as creepy as she imagined.

"Well, are you going to open the boxes to see if you like what's inside?"

"I already had a few dresses I could have worn to a fancy dinner party. You didn't have to buy me anything."

"Open the box, Kaia."

She figured the faster she did as he requested, the sooner she could get rid of him. She opened the box and gasped. Inside was a red chiffon dress. The material looked shimmery. She picked it up and held it up to the light. It was almost translucent but with the right undergarments, she would be able to maintain her modesty. It was beautiful and Kaia was certain it cost more than any item of clothing she'd ever owned. She ran her fingers over the soft material.

"Do you like it?"

"It's beautiful but you shouldn't have."

"But, I wanted to. I want to see you in the items that I buy. I want to see you dressed up in the clothing I purchase for you. You deserved to be dressed in the finest silks and satins."

"You make me sound like a kept woman."

He placed his hands on her shoulders and pressed a kiss against the nape of her neck. "You're my woman. Don't ever forget that."

And, that's what frightened the hell out of her.

Chapter Twelve

Blaise seemed to have thought of everything. Right down to her hair and makeup. He'd had someone come over to help her get ready for the dinner party and Kaia couldn't help but wonder what kind of gathering this would be. Or was this simply how rich people lived? A girl could get used to being pampered, were it not for the psycho who was blackmailing her to be with him.

She absently touched the diamond choker, she wore around her neck. Kaia couldn't imagine how much it must have cost Blaise but she felt like an impostor wearing something this ostentatious. To anyone else, this was a beautiful piece of jewelry, but when Blaise put it on her before they left for their event, she felt like a pet and he was laying ownership to her.

She only hoped she could make it through the night without doing or saying something to embarrass herself.

Three months, she told herself. That's the soonest Aneka would get her surgery according to her nurse, Barbara. The first consultation would be next week and if all went well, the doctor could put Aneka on his schedule.

Then, she could leave and never look back.

Blaise tapped away on his cellphone as they rode in the back of yet another one of his luxury vehicles. Kaia just stared out the window. It was times like these when she wished her mother was here. She could use someone to talk to and her mother had always been a good listener and gave great advice.

"That seems to be a favorite pastime of yours," Blaise spoke, breaking into her thoughts.

"Excuse me?"

"Staring out the window. You seem to do that quite a bit whenever we're going somewhere."

"I tend to do that when I don't really have anything to say."

"Oh, I'm sure we could find plenty to talk about. I'd like to get to know you better."

A humorless laugh escaped her lips. "Is that right? Usually, that part happens before the blackmail. Besides, I'm sure you already know all you need to know about me from one of your files."

Blaise didn't respond right away. "There's plenty I learned about you from the investigation I've had done on you, but I'd rather hear it from the source. You know the power is yours to make this experience as pleasant or as unpleasant as you like, and I don't wish to fight with you."

Considering everything he'd done up to this point, Kaia had no desire to play nice but he had a point. She didn't want to spend the next few months sulking and if she could stay focused on her countdown to the day when she could get away from him, things wouldn't be so bad.

She turned to him, "I like looking out the window because I don't get to travel by car that much. I usually take the train everywhere and taking taxis' and ubers start to add up after a while. It's always been a dream of mine to come to New York, even I was a little girl. And now that I'm here, I sometimes feel like pinching myself because I can't believe I'm actually here."

"It's an interesting city." Blaise didn't sound the least bit impressed.

"The way you said that makes me think you don't like New York that much."

"I like it just fine. It's just that when you've seen one large city you've seen them all."

"I hope I never become as jaded as you. Look at this place. I mean take a really good look. What do you see?"

"Crowds, pollution and a bunch of buildings."

She shook her head at his cynicism. "When I look at this city, I see a work of art. It's perfect. I mean it may have its problems, but look at all the beautiful people. There are people from all walks of life, different races and cultures. And then, there's the lights. I've never been in a place where the night light shines as bright."

"Try Vegas."

She shook her head refusing to let him tarnish her image of her most favorite city on the planet. "This place is just so full of life and vitality. It has art, the best food, and landmarks. I can't think of a more perfect place to be."

"Perhaps, you need to see more of the world, Kaia."

She shrugged. "Maybe, but this place will always be my number one."

"While I may not agree that this is the best city in the world, hearing you speak of it, makes this place seem like a dream come true."

"It is. When my mom was alive..." she broke off. Kaia had rarely mentioned her mother to Landon. Now that she thought about it, the main reason was that he never seemed interested.

Blaise touched her hand gently. "What were you about to say about your mother?"

"I was just going to say, when my mother was alive, every Christmas instead of exchanging elaborate gifts, we'd drive up here and stay at a nice hotel, ice skate at the Rockefeller Center rink and drink hot chocolate. Then, we'd take pictures in front of the big Christmas tree. And, we'd always end the weekend with a show at Radio City Music Hall. That was my favorite. I knew then, that this is where I wanted to be when I got older."

"That sounds lovely. Sounds like you were very close to your mother."

"I was. She was my best friend. What about your parents? I mean...I assume that they're no longer alive since you have Aneka. I mean, you don't have to talk about them, if you don't want to."

"I had a good relationship with my parents. They were too good for this world, actually."

"What do you mean?"

"My father worked very hard to make his business a success and that meant taking on a partner. An unscrupulous one, who didn't like that my father wanted to pay a fair wage and look out for all of his employees. His business partner took a more capitalist approach. Mr. Nielsen and my father bumped heads and Nielsen decided to settle the argument his way."

Kaia noticed Blaise's fists balled in his lap. "What do you mean by that?"

"I don't believe my parent's car malfunctioning was an accident, but it's one of those things you could never prove."

"Oh, my goodness. I'm so sorry to hear that. What happened to Mr. Nielsen?"

"He's no longer with us," Blaise stated firmly in a tone that indicated this line of conversation was over. Kaia was certain she didn't want to know how Nielsen died because the less she knew the better. But, it did make the mystery that surrounded Blaise even more frightening.

For the rest of the ride, they remained silent until they reached their destination.

When Kaia would have gotten out the car herself, Blaise grasped her by the wrist and shook his head. "It's my honor to open the door for you, wherever we go."

"I'm quite capable—"

"I'm not arguing with you about this."

Blaise slid out of the car before coming around to open the door for her. As they walked into the building, he wrapped his arm around her shoulders and held her close. Kaia resisted the urge to pull away. She wasn't used to being held so possessively. Blaise's hand rested on her hip, leaving no doubt to anyone regarding the intimacy of their relationship.

Kaia trembled slightly as they rode the elevator to the top floor. "There's no need to be nervous."

"I'm not sure what to expect."

"For the most part, you'll stay by my side and if by some chance the two of us get separated, just smile and nod.

They were shown into a penthouse suite that was nice but wasn't quite as large as Blaise's place. It was still nicer than anywhere she'd ever lived.

Kaia looked around to see most of the men in attendance were older gentlemen dressed in suits, while the ladies were off in the corner in various states of dress.

A stout bald man approached them with a large smile on his face. He spoke to Blaise in what Kaia assumed was Danish. Blaise answered before turning to Kaia. "English, please. Peter, this is my lovely date, Kaia. Kaia, this is Peter Sorensen."

The older man looked down at Kaia and gave her a smile that made her skin crawl. He took her hand and pressed fleshy lips on her knuckles. "Charmed." He turned to Blaise. "You always did have great taste in women, although Lisbeth will be quite displeased. Oh well, 'you win some, you lose some', as the Americans say. I must go entertain my other guests but please have a drink at the bar and partake in the hors d' oeuvres."

No sooner did Peter walk away when a tall blonde with huge breasts approached. She was almost eye level with Blaise, making Kaia feel like a shrimp at 5'4".

Completely ignoring Kaia, the blonde threw her arms around Blaise and attempted to kiss him. Blaise, however, seemed perturbed at the attempt.

"Lisbeth, show a little decorum."

The woman spoke to Blaise in their native tongue, excluding Kaia who had no idea what was going on. It was clear the blonde had a thing for Blaise. He nodded in Kaia's direction before asking the woman to speak English.

The blonde finally turned her attention to Kaia and Kaia felt like a bug under a microscope. Kaia raised her chin and stared back.

Without a word, the woman rolled her eyes and walked away.

"Wow, that was an interesting exchange."

"Ignore her. Lisbeth is an acquired taste."

"Former lover?"

"Regretfully, yes. Are you jealous?"

"Of what? It's not like we're really together."

"You keep telling yourself that, *kæreste*."

The remainder of the evening was uneventful. Kaia stayed by Blaise's side for the most part. She'd even had a few conversations with the wives of the men. One of the women asked what she did for a living and when she said she was a dancer that had sparked a pleasant conversation. Her only issue with the evening was the fact that Lisbeth shot daggers her way whenever their eyes locked.

It wasn't her fault that Blaise no longer wanted her. Kaia figured there would be no problems as long as the blonde didn't say anything to her, but that was exactly what happened when Kaia excused herself to go to the bathroom. When she came out, Lisbeth was standing by the door.

Kaia attempted to walk by the blonde but Lisbeth grasped her by the arm, digging her nails into her skin.

"Excuse you." She looked pointedly at the pale hand gripping her arm.

"I'd like a word with you," the haughty blonde replied, still holding on to Kaia's arm.

"And, I'd like for you take your hand off of me." Kaia didn't consider herself a violent person but this lady had two seconds to remove her hand.

"And, if I don't?" Lisbeth challenged.

"Keep holding me and find out." She clenched her fists at her side and glared up at her adversary.

Lisbeth must have noticed the motion because she released Kaia and smirked. "So violent, but I suppose that's what one would expect of your kind."

"My kind?" Was this bitch for real?

"You know exactly what I'm talking about. You don't belong here. Blaise may dress you up and give you expensive baubles," she sneered, eyeing Kaia's diamond choker, "but you'll never fit in. No one will accept you."

Kaia was a black woman in America, so she'd heard far worse from people who were much better at this game than Lisbeth. It was clear the blonde was jealous because she was with Blaise and in her paltry attempt to intimidate Kaia, Lisbeth was making a complete ass of herself.

"Are you finished?" Kaia asked bored with this woman's inane babbling.

"I just thought I'd offer you a little friendly advice is all. Blaise is mine. He may keep you around as his little plaything for a little while but he'll eventually tire of you, and when he does, he'll come back to someone with class."

Kaia couldn't help but laugh. If this wasn't so pathetic, she'd actually be upset. "Someone with class? Then that person clearly isn't you. How sad are you that you're going after a man who clearly doesn't want you? Maybe you should be having your little chat with Blaise, instead of me. Have a little self-respect."

"Why you little—"

"Is there a problem?" Blaise appeared as if by magic. He slid his arm around Kaia's waist and held her close. For the first time, she was actually thankful for his presence because a few seconds later and she was almost certain she would have kicked Lisbeth in the face.

Lisbeth's expression instantly changed from a sneer to a seductive smile. The transformation was so quick, Kaia was wondering if she'd just imagined the confrontation. "There's no problem at all, Blaise. Me and Kia were just having a little girls', chat." She looked at Kaia as if daring her to say otherwise.

It was on the tip of Kaia's tongue to tell this bitch about herself but Blaise spoke before she had a chance. "Her name is Kaia, not Kia."

Lisbeth placed her hand over her mouth in mock embarrassment. "Oh, my. I'm so sorry. I'm so terrible with names. Forgive me." It was so fake Kaia wanted to gag.

Blaise, however, didn't seem the least bit amused. "Lisbeth, I've known you for longer than I care to admit and as for as I've seen, you've never mispronounced anyone's name. And to do so now, makes you look petty and small-minded. It's the very reason why I ended our association and why I never intend to renew it. You see, I heard everything you said to Miss Benson, I just wanted to give you more rope to hang yourself with and you didn't disappoint. Kaia has more class in her pinky finger than you have in your entire surgically enhanced body. Now, I suggest you stay out of my way and *my woman's* way. That's right, she's mine and I intend for it to remain that way."

Lisbeth's mouth fell open and this time her embarrassment was genuine.

"Blaise, how can you say these things to me? Especially, when we've meant so much to each other."

"Your memory must be failing you again because clearly, that's not how things were. You were an occasional hostess at my functions and lover. There were no deep feelings between us."

"But I...I love you." Tears swam in the blonde's eyes.

"You don't love me, Lisbeth. You love what I can do for you. The only person you're capable of loving is yourself. Perhaps, I should cease doing business with your father, even though his company can't exactly afford to take another hit with the way things have been going at Sorensen's."

"You wouldn't."

"Don't test me, Lisbeth. Goodnight."

"Blaise..."

"I said, goodnight." Blaise pulled Kaia away from the blonde who looked as if she were about to cry at any moment. Kaia almost felt sorry for the other woman, almost. But, fuck her.

After that encounter, Kaia was more than ready to leave this gathering. These kinds of events weren't exactly her thing. Thankfully, Blaise was of the same mind. They made their rounds and said their goodbyes before leaving.

When they were in the car, Kaia turned to him. "I could have handled her."

"I'm sure you could have but Lisbeth needed to hear a few home truths. She's the kind of person who will continue to pursue something relentlessly even when it's unobtainable."

Kaia couldn't help but laugh at Blaise's audacity. How could he not see the irony of his words? "Kind of like you?"

"Not at all like me. Because unlike, Lisbeth, when I go after something...or someone, I get it."

And just like that, any goodwill she'd felt toward him vanished with his arrogant declaration. "Well, you can't have me," she snapped.

"But, I already have you. And by the end of the night that will mean, in every way possible."

Chapter Thirteen

Blaise Lundgaard was crazy if he thought she was going to be so easily seduced by him. When they entered the penthouse, everything was quiet which meant that Aneka and Barbara were in bed. Kaia made a beeline for the stairs hoping to make it to her room and lock the door firmly behind her before Blaise could enact his crazy plan. But instead of following her as she thought he would, he headed for the bar.

"There's no need to rush off Kaia. Have a drink with me."

She shook her head. "I'm tired and I'd like to lie down. Besides, I have to get up early in the morning. Hopefully, I won't get bombarded with questions by everyone after the way you made an ass of yourself at the studio."

He smiled as he poured himself a drink. He seemed completely unbothered by what she'd just said. "I'll be up shortly. Take everything off except the choker."

Kaia narrowed her eyes. It was apparent he was trying to get a rise out of her and she wasn't going to take the bait. Instead of dignifying that command with a response she rolled her eyes. She locked the door once she was inside her bedroom.

The first thing she did was take off the choker and place it on her dresser drawer. Afterwards, Kaia washed the makeup off her face, undressed and took a long hot shower. The hot spray of the water helped her aching muscles. They felt slightly strained because she didn't stretch properly before practice.

The dinner party had only added to her stress. Sure, the attendees were polite and smiled in her face but she could read the message in their eyes. Lisbeth was right, she didn't belong among those people. Maybe Blaise would eventually see that as well, and end this charade, sooner rather than later.

Feeling refreshed, she wrapped the towel around her body and headed to her bedroom.

"Oh my god!" Kaia squealed when she encountered Blaise sitting on her bed holding the choker in his hand. "How the hell did you get in here? I locked the door."

"Kaia, you disobeyed an order. I wanted you to leave the choker on. That was naughty of you."

"Get out!" She pointed to the door with one hand and held the towel against her as tightly as possible with the other.

"Do you know what happens when people disobey orders? They get punished. What kind of punishment do you think you deserve?"

"I said get out or I'll scream."

Blaise stroked the choker. "One of the reasons, I bought this property was the excellent soundproofing. This particular penthouse used to be owned by a musician. He's in the Rock N' Roll Hall of Fame from my understanding. You may have heard of him. But never mind that. My point is, that you can scream to your heart's content. In fact, I welcome it, although I'd prefer that you're using my name when you do it."

Kaia only suspected that Blaise was unhinged before but now she was certain. She took several steps backward. "Blaise, I'm tired and I'd like to go to bed. I'm not in the mood to play these games with you."

"Who's playing games? I'm not. I had one request; that you be waiting for me with nothing but this." He held up the choker and stalked toward her, a determined look in his icy gaze.

Kaia moved backward until her back hit the wall. She clung even tighter to the towel. She shook her head as he boxed her in, placing his hands on either side of her head. "Turn around, so I can put it on you."

Her heart beat so fast, she thought it would burst out of her chest. This man terrified and excited her at the same time. Kaia wasn't certain if that made her a little crazy for feeling this way.

Escape was necessary so she wouldn't succumb to this madness. Quickly, Kaia ducked under his arms and headed to the bathroom but for a large man, Blaise was quick. He captured her by the arm and whirled her around. The next thing Kaia knew, Blaise tossed her over his shoulder.

"Put me, down, you creep!" She pounded her fists against his back but it seemed to have little effect on him. He carried Kaia out of her bedroom and down the hallway until they reached a different one. It was the master bedroom which was twice the size of her accommodations. The whole room was shrouded in gold and black but she didn't have a chance to take in the décor before he tossed her on the center of the bed.

Kaia immediately scrambled to her knees and searched the room for any possible exits.

Blaise, however, seemed to be in no hurry as he casually walked to the bedroom door and locked it.

There was a balcony but they were on top of a twenty story building. She could run to his bathroom and lock herself in but Blaise had already proven to be too quick for her.

She watched warily as Blaise pushed a button on the side of a full-length mirror that adorned his wall. It turned out the mirror was a sliding glass door that revealed his closet.

Blaise pressed another button and a row of ties popped forward. He selected four of them before turning to her. As he slowly made his way to the bed, it dawned on Kaia what he intended to do with them. And all the while, he held on to the choker.

Shit, even if she didn't have a chance to escape, the least she could do was try. Rolling off the bed, she raced to the door. She managed to get her fingers around the doorknob before Blaise pulled her back. She kicked and screamed with all her strength but he was much too strong for her.

"Let me go! I don't want this! You promised that I wouldn't have to do anything I didn't want."

Blaise remained eerily silent which only made her fight harder. She even made her body go limp to make it difficult for him to get her to the bed but he lifted her as if she weighed nothing to him.

Once again, she found herself tossed on the bed but this time Blaise captured one of her wrists. She tried to pull away from him but somehow, he managed to wrap the tie around her wrist and form a knot. He then took the other end of the tie and tied it to one bedpost.

"Stop this!" She smacked his arm and any part of him she could get her free hand on. Kaia realized that if he was able to secure her other wrist, then her chance of escaping was slim to none. Before he could grab her other arm. She raked her nails down the side of his face.

He inhaled sharply and focused his gaze on her. His light-colored eyes had darkened but his expression remained unreadable. "That's going to cost you."

He was too strong for her as he tied her other arm to the post. Kaia screamed as loud as she could, hoping that her voice could penetrate the soundproofing. No one came to her rescue.

She tried to kick him as he worked to secure her legs to the foot of the bed with the ties. By the time he was finished, the towel had long since fallen away and she was spread wide for his lascivious gaze.

She struggled against her restraints but Blaise had done a good job of securing her. "This is rape!" she screamed.

A sinister smile curved Blaise's lips. "You think so? Interesting." Instead of joining her on the bed like Kaia thought he would, he picked up the choker that had fallen to the floor.

As he got closer, she noticed the scratch marks on his cheek, marring an otherwise perfect face. In most circumstances, she would have regretted doing something like that to another human being. But in this case, she wished she'd done more.

"Hold your head up for me," he instructed.

Refusing to cooperate, she glared at him hoping she could convey every bit of hate she felt for him at that moment.

"Suit yourself." He gripped her by the hair and lifted her head long enough to slip the choker around her neck. He then released her hair and fastened the clip with both hands. "Perfect."

He pulled away and stared at her as if he was admiring a painting in a gallery.

"I hate you."

"Do you hate me or do you hate that in a bit, I'm going to make you feel things you didn't know possible?"

"Fuck you," she said between clenched teeth.

"That's the intention, *kæreste*. But hold that thought."

To her surprise, he left the room.

While he was gone, Kaia fought and struggled against her bonds, but to no avail. He'd tied her in too tightly and her wrists and ankles were getting sore from the struggling.

Blaise returned shortly, closing the door behind him with a decisive click. In one hand he held a bottle of amber liquor and a glass. He walked to the desk in the corner of the room and pulled the chair from it before dragging it next to the bed. He sat down and as calm as he pleased, he poured himself a glass of the liquor. Slowly he placed the bottle on the floor next to him and took a sip. As he did all this, his eyes never left her.

Kaia had never felt this exposed in her life and there had been a play in her college where all the performers had to go topless at one point. That had just been a performance. This was something on a whole other level of kinky. Goosebumps formed on her skin as he skimmed her body with that intense gaze of his. She barely managed not to shiver. She made another attempt to break her ties only to receive a chuckle from Blaise

"You're insane, do you know that? When I get out of these restraints, I'm leaving and never coming back, damn the consequences."

Blaise took another sip of his drink before answering. "Good to know. I guess that means I'm going to have to keep you tethered to my bed for the rest of your life. I mean, it would be quite uncomfortable for me to sleep on that bed with you spread out like that, but I think we can make it work," he stated before bringing the glass to his lips again.

"You can't be serious," she whispered as her heart sped up once again.

"Of course not. As much as I would love to have you like this always: with your beautiful little titties sitting high and your legs spread wide, showing off that delectable cunt, waiting for me to be inside of it, it simply wouldn't be practical."

Kaia shook her head from side to side. "Please don't do this. Remember the contract."

He shrugged one shoulder with a nonchalance that made her want to scream. That he could be so casual about this situation was pissing her off. "The contract we both signed. You promised me that we wouldn't...have sex until I was ready."

"The contract doesn't say that. How do you think it would have looked if I were to present my lawyer with something like that? An agreement based on sex would never hold up in court, but what will is that I promised to fund your ex's little dance company, you continue to dance and I leave your friends alone. In exchange, you would be my companion for a set amount of time. And if either of us were to back out then we'd have a breach of contract. Did you not read through the entire document?"

She'd skimmed through it but hadn't read every single line. Kaia had simply assumed… "But you said, you wouldn't touch me until I was ready."

"You were ready from the moment you walked into my home, and I'm not talking about after the agreement was made. I mean the night of the party. Oh, you'll probably deny it because you were still cozied up to that man-boy. You might have thought you were in love with him but he couldn't satisfy you. Or else you wouldn't have burst into flames the second I touched you. The attraction was there the second our eyes locked and this moment here? What you may label as force or even rape, I say it's inevitable. And I'm going to enjoy proving it to you."

"You may have me tied up, but you can't make me like it."

"Of course not, my dear. I won't make you like it. I'm going to make you love it. I'm going to make you crave it. I'm going to make you need it. I'm going to make you beg for it."

His words made her body quiver, much to her chagrin. "In your dreams."

Blaise smirked. "You've been in my dreams since the moment I saw you. But now it will very much become a reality. Do you know what this is?" He held up the glass.

Kaia glared at him not dignifying his nonsensical question with an answer.

"This is one of the finest brandys made in Europe. I was just wondering if the taste would be enhanced against your skin." He dipped his finger into the liquid, leaned forward and circled her nipple.

Kaia squeezed her eyes shut, trying to stave off any feelings of pleasure, but the slow seductive movements of his finger made her nipple pebble beneath his touch. Blaise repeated the motion giving her other breast the same attention.

She bit her bottom lip to hold back the moan in the back of her throat. Before she realized what was happening, she felt the bed depress and her nipple was engulfed in his warm hot mouth. He sucked aggressively, tugging and nibbling the sensitive tip until Kaia found herself arching her back.

When he bit down on the turgid tip she cried out. "Oh!"

Blaise released her nipple with a loud wet pop. "Delicious. My drink tastes even better on your body." He sucked and nibbled on each breast in turn.

"Please don't do this to me," she whispered, even as heat coursed through her body.

"I must," he moaned, burying his face against her neck. He sucked the area above her collarbone so roughly, she was certain there would be a mark in the morning. Despite wanting desperately to resist his passionate onslaught, her pussy tingled and her juices slid down her inner thighs.

She hated that he could do this to her, make her want him to not stop, but Kaia didn't dare vocalize this. She refused to let him win.

Blaise pulled away from her and she opened her eyes to see him grab the glass of brandy. He then poured the liquid down the center of her body.

"What are you doing?" she groaned.

He smirked. "I'm not finished with my drink. Blaise ran his tongue from the valley of her breasts to her tummy, stopping before he reached the junction of her thighs. He poured more liquor on her belly, slurping it from the hollow of her navel. "By the time I'm finished with this, I think I'm going be well and truly hungover, but not from the brandy."

Kaia pulled against her restraints, unable to keep still. She hated that he could do this to her and that it felt so good. She raised her hips, silently pleading for him to ease her ache.

"So anxious. You want this don't you?"

Kaia turned her head away from him, refusing to tell him the words he wanted to hear.

Blaise poured the remaining contents of his glass between her legs.

"Oh God!" she cried at the tickle of the liquid hitting her clit.

"He's not here, kæreste. But I can take you to heaven tonight," he said settling himself between her thighs.

He ran his finger down her slit and parted her tender folds. "Such a beautiful cunt, all wet and pink and look at your little friend peeking out to say hello." He flicked her clit and Kaia nearly lost it.

"Bl..." she stopped short of calling out his name making him laugh.

"So close. That's fine, the night is still young"

He lowered himself and placed his mouth over her pussy. He didn't simply lick her and suck, he devoured. His mouth and tongue were everywhere tasting her in places that have never been explored before. He ate her pussy until her eyes crossed. Kaia bucked her hips against her mouth, unable to remain still.

"Blaise!" she screamed his name involuntarily.

He parted her ass cheeks and licked her rosette, circling it before returning to her sex. He then shoved his tongue into her pussy.

Kaia rode his face as she got closer to her climax.

And then he abruptly pulled away.

Kaia whimpered. She had been so close.

Obsessed

"You don't get to come until you beg for it."

Chapter Fourteen

Blaise could see the warring emotions cross her lovely face. He'd never seen a more beautiful sight than Kaia, spread out for him; her pussy on display, her inner thighs wet with her juices. Her nipples, which were the color of blackberries, were erect and her bottom lip was swollen from her biting it.

His cock was so fucking hard that he wanted to take her right here and now, but he needed to hear her say the words. That she wanted him. Admittedly, his ego was a little bruised when she'd told him that she'd never give in to him. Proving her wrong had become a mission for him. By the end of the night, he wanted there to be no doubt in her mind who she belonged to.

She wouldn't meet his gaze.

"Look at me, Kaia."

She kept her eyes averted.

"Look at me or else, I'm going to eat your pussy again and stop just before you come. And then, I'm going to watch you squirm and do it all over again, denying you your release. Now, fucking look at me!" roared.

Kaia finally looked him in the eyes. "Don't make me say it."

"Say what? The truth? I would have thought you'd have learned by now that I don't make empty threats."

Blaise proceeded to untie her ankles so he could have better access to her cunt. He returned to the bed and placed her legs over his shoulders and proceeded to devour her. This time, as he sucked on her clit, he slid two fingers into her tight sheath, knuckles deep.

Kaia wiggled and gyrated her hips, yet she still didn't say the words he wanted to hear.

The second he felt her body seize up, signaling her orgasm was imminent, he pulled away yet again.

She screamed, a sound of pure frustration.

"We can play this game all night."

Kaia's only response was to glare at him, so he pulled back and waited until her body had relaxed once again. And then, he proceeded to tongue fuck her hot box.

This went on a few more times, Blaise feasting on her delectable cunt taking her to the point of completion and then pulling back.

The fourth time, as he proceeded to nibble on her clit Kaia cried out, "Please Blaise, let me come. I want you!"

With that small victory behind him, he sucked on her swollen nubbin and slid his fingers in and out of her until she squirted her juices in his face.

Blaise took his time licking her clean. He could have remained between her legs for hours but his dick was painfully hard and if he didn't get relief, he might go insane.

He rolled off the bed and quickly undressed, tossing his clothing to the side. Blaise noticed the way her eyes roamed his body. He took pride in his physique which he worked hard to maintain.

"Do you like what you, see, Kaia?"

"Yes. But I'm sure you already know that you have a nice body."

"Not as nice as yours." He moved to the side of the bed and undid one wrist and then went to the other side of the bed to free the other one. Kaia immediately rubbed her wrists but Blaise took them in his hands, noticing the red rings around her skin. He kissed the irritated area before settling himself on top of her.

"You're mine now, Kaia, and there's no turning back after tonight," he warned her as he nudged her legs apart and positioned his cock at her entrance.

"You're not wearing protection," she protested weakly.

"Nor do I intend to. You're mine and there will be no barriers between us."

"But—"

"There will be no barrier between us," he growled before thrusting into her. Kaia was already so wet that he was able to dive in balls deep with virtually no resistance.

He could feel her tightness when he had put his fingers inside of her. But that hadn't prepared him for the way her walls clenched his dick so tightly, he doubted he'd be able to hold out for long.

He felt as if she was made especially for him, like a warm velvety hug.

Obsessed

"Wrap your legs around me, kæreste," he moaned as he planted his hands on either side of her head and started to move in and out of her. With each thrust, he went deeper and harder. Blaise had imagined this moment for so long, but the reality was far better than his dreams. Everything about this woman turned him on, from the little kitten sounds she made in the back of her throat to the way she ran her nails down his chest.

Unlike many lovers he'd had, she wasn't the kind of woman who just lay beneath him like a cold lump. No, not his Kaia. She raised her hips up to meet his dick, every time he plowed into her.

Blaise did his best to hold out as long as he could, but her pussy was just too good. "Mine!" roared before shooting his seed inside of her. A primitive part of him wished that one of them would take root and make a baby, but he knew she was on birth control. Little did Kaia know, she wouldn't be for long. He was playing for keeps.

"I need to come," Kaia begged.

"Don't hold back."

"Oh, yeah," she groaned as her entire body shook. Her mouth fell open and her eyes rolled to the back of her head. The very sight of Kaia hitting her climax, made him want to take her all over again but the night was still young and Kaia looked as if she was about to fall asleep.

Blaise rolled off her and pulled her against him. He would let her rest, for now.

Kaia was so exhausted that she could barely keep her eyes open. She'd barely gotten any sleep the night before. Blaise had been insatiable. They'd had sex throughout most of the night. After one sexual romp, Kaia drifted off, only to later be awaked with Blaise inside of her.

Once, she'd woke up with his head between her legs. Another time, he was sucking on her breast. The man was a sexual demon of some sort because this morning, he barely seemed phased.

Though he suggested that she sleep in, Kaia didn't want to be late for another rehearsal, especially after what happened the day before. Besides, she couldn't spend the rest of the day in the penthouse, because then she'd have too much free time on her hands. And the more of that she had, the more she would think about what happened between her and Blaise.

It still felt so surreal. She'd been so determined to deny him access to her body but just as Blaise had declared she would, Kaia had begged him to take her. She was ashamed that she allowed that to happen to her, and that she actually liked it. What was wrong with her? She had just gotten out of a long-term relationship, only to find herself in bed with another man soon after.

She could tell herself that it was because he'd practically forced her, but deep down Kaia knew that wasn't exactly true. She hated Blaise but he still turned her on in ways that no man ever had. And if she was being honest, after being with Blaise, she could admit that the sex between her and Landon had been lackluster. Most of the time, if he climaxed before her that would be it, but Kaia had never complained.

Being with Blaise was an experience all on its own. She was still annoyed that he refused to use a condom. Thank goodness she was on birth control because there was no way she was going to have that demon's baby.

"We're here, Miss. Bennet," Roger spoke from the driver's seat.

Kaia had been so deep in thought, she didn't notice that they'd arrived at their destination. It was going to take some getting used to, being chauffeured everywhere, especially when she had grown accustomed to taking the subway or walking all over the city. But, Blaise had insisted that she use one of his drivers wherever she went.

When Kaia walked into the studio, most of the dancers were already there. Most of them gave her curious looks as she slid out of her sweats and started to stretch. Kaia endured stares and whispers for most of the morning. Even Landon eyed her warily, but no one said anything to her. When Landon finally called a break, everyone broke off into groups and no one approached her, not so much as a hello.

Finally, Patty approached her. "Hi Kaia," she said hesitantly.

"Hi, Patty. What's going on today? Everyone is acting like I have cooties."

"I don't know, Kaia. You tell me. That was quite a scene yesterday."

Kaia sighed. This was exactly what she feared would happen when Blaise had dragged her out of the studio. "That was...it's a long story."

Patty shrugged. "Well, we have fifteen minutes before the break is over, so you might as well spill it. What's going on with you and Blaise Lundgaard? Is he the reason you and Landon broke up? After you left, Deena said she overheard Landon and Blaise fighting over you. She also said that you dumped Landon for Blaise because he has money."

Kaia looked around the room to see Deena shooting her the evil eye. *Of course, she'd said something. That woman was evil personified.*

"Patty, you know me so you should know that I'm not like that. Deena is just looking for a way to start gossip."

"But my eyes didn't deceive me when Blaise was dragging you out of the studio as if he had some kind of claim on you. And then, there's the matter of him showing up at my apartment to come get you. I know Deena is full of horseshit sometimes, but even you have to admit how things look. I saw the way that man looked at you...all possessive like. Are you having an affair with him?"

With anyone else, she would have ignored the question, but she owed Patty an explanation. After all, her friend had allowed her to crash on her couch for a couple days, no questions asked. "Do you promise you won't tell anyone else?"

"I know, I like to talk and gossip as much as the next person, but I don't tell secrets."

"Okay, maybe, we should step out into the hallway."

"Wow, this must be secretive."

When they were in the hall, Kaia looked around them to make sure there were no eavesdroppers. When she was sure they were alone, she relayed the story from her perspective, leaving out the part where Blaise had the rest of the dancers investigated. Kaia saw no point in creeping anyone else out about the situation. By the time she was finished with her tale, Patty's mouth was wide open.

"Whoa. That sounds like a movie on one of those women's channels. I can't believe that's happening to you. I mean I believe it, it's just...wow. I'm so sorry. And as for Landon, I knew he could be a selfish bastard but to do that. You've shown a lot more restraint than I ever could have."

"At the end of the day, Bodies in Motion will continue to thrive."

"But now, I feel like shit that you had to sacrifice yourself to save the company, although you could do a whole lot worse than someone like Blaise Lundgaard. The man is a walking god. He's hot and he's rich. If a hot billionaire propositioned me, I'd ask where I could sign up. The only men who ever hit on me, are those weird guys on my block who keep catcalling me and the cashier at my local bodega."

Kaia remained silent as her friend rambled. She knew Patty meant well, but this little pep talk of hers wasn't helping the situation.

Patty must have realized that as well because she blushed. "I'm sorry. There I go, running my mouth, again. You shouldn't have been put in that position in the first place."

"Thank you."

"But like you said, it's only temporary until his sister has her surgery and then, they'll be heading back to Denmark."

"That's correct but then again, he never explicitly said he was moving back to Europe just that I had to stick around until after the surgery.'

"And when is that?"

"A few months from now. I'm sorry that I have to nix the idea of us rooming together. I can't expect you to wait a few months before I can move out of Blaise's home."

"Oh, I forgot to tell you. My father interviewed for that position that Blaise suggested and he got the job. And the best part is, he'll be making significantly more money. Of course, it would require him and mom to move closer to the office but the cost of living is a little cheaper in the town they have their eye on. So, it all worked out."

It seemed to be working out for everyone else but her, but she didn't want to begrudge her friend her good news. "I'm happy to hear that. Well, it looks like the break is over."

Kaia's shoulder slumped. She dreaded going back inside.

Patty put her arm around her. "If anyone says something, I'll shut it down."

"Thanks, Patty, I appreciate it but I can handle myself."

"Well, just know that I have you back."

"At least someone does."

Chapter Fifteen

"I've gone over Aneka's files and it looks like everything is in order. If all the tests we've done today look good, we can go ahead and schedule your sister for surgery by the end of the summer," Dr. Jefferson smiled at them as he closed the file.

"And that means I'll be able to walk again."

"I can't give you a 100% guarantee but I can say that this procedure has a high success rate among my patients."

"But if the surgery works, how soon will I be able to dance?" Aneka insisted.

Blaise chuckled and patted his sister on the hand. "You have to learn how to walk again before you can dance."

"Your brother is right. After the surgery, it can take up to a few weeks before you start getting the feeling back in your legs. After that, you'd need to undergo an extensive amount physical therapy," the doctor confirmed.

"Oh," Aneka said slumping in her chair.

"I'm sure if all goes well, you'll be dancing in no time," the doctor assured her.

"I'd like that very much," Aneka's grin returned. She then turned to Kaia, who had sat silently through the consultation at Aneka's request. "And, will you teach me to dance like you."

"I can't teach you to dance like me, but I can teach you to dance like you. And, I'm sure you'll dance beautifully."

This response seemed to make the child smile. "I can't wait!"

"Do any of you have any more questions?" The doctor inquired.

Blaise fired off a series of questions which Dr. Jefferson answered competently. It was clear Blaise cared deeply for his sister, but it was hard to reconcile this loving father figure to the ruthless brute she knew him to be when it came to her.

Kaia had lived with Blaise and Aneka for a week now and she was still getting used to it. After their night together, Blaise had had Kaia's stuff moved to his room and when Kaia protested, he'd run roughshod over her. And, every night since had been filled with sex. The part that made Kaia so uneasy was the fact that she welcomed it, though she'd never admit it out loud. It was almost as if the man had put some kind of spell on her and she was his willing sex slave.

Obsessed

Thankfully, there had been no more dinner parties thus far. Another thing she was grateful for, was the fact she only saw him in the evenings because he was usually at the office and Kaia was at the studio rehearsing for their show's opening in two weeks.

The atmosphere had been filled tension those first few days at the studio with the other dancers, but it soon settled down. Her friends didn't ask questions and Kaia had no desire to talk about it, so the subject was never brought up. The only flies in her ointment were Deena and Landon. Deena was still resentful over the fact that Kaia had the lead in the biggest dance number. While Landon would shoot her resentful stares as if she were the one to mess things up between them.

Those two seemed to be getting close. Kaia wasn't sure what was going on with those two, but she was determined to not let either one of them get under her skin.

After the doctor's visit, Aneka asked if they could go out to lunch together, which Blaise agreed to.

Kaia sent off a quick text to Landon to let him know that she would be at rehearsal later than she anticipated. She had become especially sensitive about punctuality because half the dance troupe believed she was getting special perks because of her relationship with Blaise. Never mind that she'd already had the principal dance spot long before Blaise had come into the picture or the fact that she worked hard to get where she was. It sucked that all of her hard work was being questioned because of something she'd had no control over.

'Who are you texting?" Blaise asked.

"Landon. I was telling him that I'd be later than I told him I'd be because we're going to lunch."

The muscle in his jaw twitched and she could tell that he wasn't pleased, but thankfully he didn't say anything further about it because Aneka began to chatter blissfully unaware of the tension in the car.

The restaurant they chose was a small quaint restaurant in Little Italy that served the best Spaghetti Bolognese.

When they were seated and their orders were taken, Aneka leaned over the table to whisper to Kaia. "Thank you so much for coming with me today. I was scared."

"Why?" Kaia asked. "You did fantastically."

"I was worried that the doctor would give me bad news and I just wanted to have the extra support."

"Well, it was my pleasure. You're going to walk again Aneka. You've got to believe that." Kaia squeezed the pre-teen's hand to reassure her.

Aneka gave her a bright smile. "You know, I like the three of us together. We feel like a family."

Kaia was in the middle of taking a sip of her water and nearly choked on it when Aneka said that.

"Are you okay?" The girl frowned.

"Uh, yeah, I think my water went down the wrong pipe."

Blaise didn't bother to hide his amusement. "It does feel nice having the three of us together. Aneka wouldn't you like it if we made this a permanent arrangement?"

Aneka nodded. "I'd love that. Kaia is so nice and pretty. She's not like your other girlfriends, especially Lisbeth." She made a gagging face to emphasize her point.

Kaia didn't like where this conversation was headed. She didn't appreciate how Blaise was trying to manipulate her through his sister, but she didn't want Aneka to sense the tension between Kaia and her brother. "When your brother and I went to that dinner party the other week, I met Lisbeth. I can see why you're not too fond of her."

"She is the worst. I'm so glad Blaise no longer sees her,' Aneka added.

"I didn't realize you had such adverse feelings toward Lisbeth, precious," Blaise chimed in. "Why did you never say anything?"

Aneka shrugged. "Because you liked her and I didn't want to upset you."

"Aneka, you must know that you could never upset me over something like that. When our parents died, I vowed to take care of you and make sure you wanted for nothing, and that includes your happiness. If something is bothering you, then you should speak up."

"Thank you, Blaise. It doesn't matter now because we don't have to worry about Lisbeth anymore and now, you're with Kaia."

Kaia needed a break. She had to get away from this conversation. Abruptly, she stood. "Uh, I have to go to the restroom. When the waiter returns, could you please have him refill my water glass?" Without waiting for either Blaise or Aneka to answer, she hurried away from the table and into the bathroom. It was single occupancy, so she locked the door behind her.

What the hell was going on? When Kaia had moved in with Blaise, she didn't take into account what Aneka would think about the situation, but apparently, the girl believed that Kaia and Blaise were in an actual relationship. It wasn't like she could burst Aneka's bubble and tell her that the only reason she was there was essentially because she was being blackmailed.

When this was all over, she would end up breaking that little girl's heart. Blaise must have known that. He was a manipulative man, so she wouldn't have put it past him to use his little sister to get what he wanted. Just when she thought he couldn't sink any lower, he managed to do just that. There had to be a way around that but she had to figure it out.

Kaia didn't know how long she was hunched over the sink contemplating her predicament when someone knocked on the bathroom door. "I'll be out in a second," she called.

She checked her appearance in the mirror and wiped the tears from the corners of her eyes. When she got herself together, she walked out to see a little old lady tapping her foot impatiently. "Well, it took you long enough," the woman muttered brushing past her.

"Have a nice day," Kaia countered shaking her head turned around and bumped into a tall dark haired man.

"Sorry about my grandmother. She hasn't eaten yet so she's a little cranky."

Kaia returned his smile. "It's okay. I was taking longer than I should have in there."

He smiled revealing a dimpled cheek. "I hope you're all right."

"I'm fine. Thank you."

"I'm Dylan, by the way." He held his hand out to her.

She took the offered hand and gave it a shake. "Kaia. Nice to meet you, Dylan."

"Pardon me for being so forward, but I swear I've seen you somewhere before."

She shrugged. "I don't know. This is a big city."

"Hmm, do you by chance live in Williamsburg?"

"I did but I recently moved."

"I live there now, maybe that's where I've seen you."

She shrugged. "Maybe."

"It's a shame you moved because I've only moved to the area to help my grandmother manage her rental properties. I don't know too many people in the area yet."

"Well, despite what everyone says about New York, there are plenty of friendly people and I'm sure you'll have no problem making friends."

"Perhaps, we can exchange numbers and hang out sometime, Kaia."

"That won't be possible. If you were thinking that Kaia was available, you are mistaken."

She didn't see Blaise approach but the sound of his voice was enough to make her shake. His words were spoken softly but the underlying steel shouted red alert.

Dylan blushed. "My apologies." He turned to Blaise. "You can't blame a man for trying. Kaia is, after all, a beautiful woman."

Blaise's only response was to stare the other man down.

Kaia wanted the floor to open up and swallow her whole.

Dylan looked away. 'Uh, well, I better go wait for my grandmother." He walked away, leaving Kaia with a tight-lipped Blaise.

Blaise took Kaia by the wrist and guided her by the tables. The food had arrived and Aneka was happily eating her pasta.

"You're back. I was wondering what was taking you so long," the girl said with a mouthful of food.

"We don't speak with our mouths full of food," Blaise lightly reprimanded his sister as he took his seat.

"Sorry." She gave him a sheepish grin.

The little appetite Kaia had had completely vanished. She'd ordered a Caesar salad with blackened chicken, and it looked and smelled delicious but she couldn't taste a thing.

For the rest of lunch, Blaise stared at her silently seeming to look right into her soul. Aneka, bless her little heart, chatted on obliviously.

By the time lunch was over, she was so tense that she couldn't wait to get to the studio to practice. Neither she nor Blaise spoke, only talking when Aneka asked them a question.

Kaia was so relieved when she finally made it to rehearsal. But it had turned out to be another ordeal. Half of the dancers were still acting weird around her and Deena wasn't even trying to hide the fact that she thought Kaia was a whore who dumped Landon for their wealthy backer. Her friends like Patty, Colin, Jackie, and Miranda still had her back.

Landon was no help. Maybe it was because of their upcoming show, but he was being a bigger taskmaster than usual. He yelled at everyone and criticized anyone making the slightest misstep. He'd even made one of the dancers cry by calling her an untalented clod.

Usually, when Landon was going on one of his tirades, Kaia had been the intermediary. She was the one who would lift everyone's spirits. But now that they were no longer together, she doubted most of the other dancers would appreciate her trying to cheer them up, especially when they believed she was the cause of Landon's bad mood.

There was one routine where she and Landon had to perform together. Though she'd managed to get through the number, he had been more aggressive in his movements; from the way, he dug his fingers into her waist whenever he had to lift her to when he pulled her against him. He was rougher than was necessary.

The end of rehearsal couldn't come soon enough and all Kaia wanted to do was go home and take a long soak in the tub. But then she remembered, she'd be going home to Blaise and suddenly going back to the penthouse didn't seem so welcoming.

"Wow, things were pretty tense in there today." Patty flopped on the floor next to Kia as she stretched.

"Yeah."

"Are you okay?"

Kaia nodded. "I'm fine."

"Look, hon, don't let what others say get to you. They don't know what they're talking about. Your real friends know that you're a good person."

"You're right. I can't be bothered with what everyone else thinks. It's just so infuriating that Landon is acting as if I was the one who wronged him."

"He's a douche canoe. He's probably upset because he realized he allowed a good thing to slip through his fingers."

Kaia shrugged. "I don't know what his problem is. Hopefully, he'll ease up once the show starts next week. It's going to be our biggest production yet and I think he said something about some major players being there to write an article on us."

Patty rolled her eyes. "There you go defending him again when he doesn't deserve it. Anyway, a few of us are going out for drinks now and you're more than welcome to come along."

Kaia wasn't really up for going out but she wasn't thrilled at the idea of facing Blaise, not after he'd made an ass of himself at lunch today. "You know what, I'd like that. Am I dressed okay?" She had put her leggings and tank top on because the weather had been nice today."

"You look fine to me."

"Great, then let's go."

Kaia called Roger to let him know that she wouldn't need a ride after rehearsal. Five minutes after she informed the driver of this, her phone rang. It was Blaise but she had no desire to talk to him so she turned her phone off.

Kaia ended up walking with her group a few blocks away to a local bar. Her little group consisted of Patty, Colin, Miranda, Jackie and another dancer, Bryan. These were the people she got on well with because they were generally a drama free crew.

Once they were at the bar, they all ordered drinks and gathered around the pool table. Kaia wasn't much of a drinker so she ordered a hard cider which she intended to nurse for the rest of her time there. After a while, she was glad she'd gone out with her friends because she found herself laughing for the first time in a while. Colin was the jokester and had them all cracking up. He poked fun of Kaia's skills at the pool table but she took it all in good fun. Kaia was having such a good time, she didn't want the night to end. So, when Miranda suggested that they try the new club a few blocks away, everyone was in except for Jackie who had to go home to tuck her kid into bed.

So, they went from a group six to five.

The club had turned out to be a dud. There were many people there and the music was bizarre but she was with her friends and they had a good time. They danced, laughed and had drinks. Since they had a rehearsal the next day, they couldn't stay out too late so they all left the club just after midnight.

Obsessed

Colin and Bryan made sure all the ladies made it to their respective rides safely. Kaia decided to splurge for an uber because she didn't feel like walking the few extra blocks to the subway.

By the time she made it back to her temporary living quarters, Kaia was tired but happy. She nodded to the doorman as he opened the door for her. The security guard at the front desk gave her a little wave.

Kaia had to punch in a code to get to Blaise's floor.

When she reached into her bag to pull out her keys, she touched her phone. Something told her to check it. Her eyes widened when she saw the screen. Thirty-seven missed calls and they'd all come from Blaise.

What in the entire fuck?

She opened the phone to see that he'd left her several text messages. Each message got progressively angrier.

Where are you, Kaia?
Why didn't you allow Roger to bring you home?
Call me.
Call me. Now!!!!
You're pissing me off, Kaia. If I have to come find you, you won't like what I'll have in store for you.
Come home now!!

She couldn't read anymore, although there had to be least twenty more texts.

Blaise was truly out of his mind. What was he thinking to call and text her so much?

Just as she got the key in the door, it was yanked open and standing before her was Blaise. But, he didn't look angry. In fact, he looked very calm.

And that's what frightened her.

Chapter Sixteen

Ever since he'd gotten that message from Roger saying that Kaia wouldn't be taking the ride home in his car, Blaise had been trying to get in contact with her. New York wasn't any more dangerous than any other major metropolitan city around the world but it didn't matter. He wanted to make sure his woman got back and forth to where she needed to go in relative safety.

When she didn't answer his call, however, he was annoyed. But as the night went on and she continued to ignore his calls and texts, he'd moved beyond that stage. At this point, he was enraged. He couldn't help imagining who she was with. Was she out with Campion? Blaise understood the break up was still fresh but he didn't think Kaia would go back on their agreement.

He wished he'd had the foresight to tell Roger to follow her but he hadn't been thinking clearly at the time. He decided first thing in the morning he would go to the cell phone store and purchase a phone. But this phone would have a special tracker installed so he would know her every move.

Long after his sister and Barbara had turned in for the night, Blaise sat in the living room with all the lights off, sipping his favorite brandy. He remembered how it had tasted on her body. He sat there allowing the rage to build within him as his imagination ran wild. Who was kissing her? Who was holding her?

It was nearly one in the morning when he heard Kaia fiddling with the lock. Blaise hopped to his feet and opened the door to see an unrepentant Kaia standing on the other side.

He stepped back to let her in careful not to touch her because he couldn't trust himself not to do something that would hurt her.

"What are you still doing up?" She asked as casually as she pleased as if he hadn't been worried sick waiting up for her.

"Where were you, Kaia?" he asked, injecting as much calm in his voice as possible.

"I was out with friends. Look, Blaise, it's late so could you please save the third degree until tomorrow. I had a nice night out and I don't want it ruined."

Something inside of him snapped. When Kaia would have walked past him, he grabbed her by the neck and pulled her back. He spun her around and slammed her against the door. "Who the fuck do you think you're talking to? *Dette er uacceptabelt!* Did you think you could fucking waltz in here with no explanation after you refused to answer my calls and texts? *Aldrig igen!*"

Her eyes widened. From the way he was slipping from English to his native tongue, she could tell he was really pissed. "Blaise, let me go."

His hand tightened around her throat. "I'm going to ask you this again. Where the fuck were you?"

She tried to pull his hand off of her but he wouldn't budge. "Please..." she wheezed.

"I'm not going to ask you again, Kaia."

"I was out with friends. A bunch of us went out for drinks and then we went dancing afterward."

"Dancing? You've been dancing all day. Did you need to dance some more?"

"We just wanted to unwind."

"And who was in this 'bunch of us'?"

"It was a few dancers from the troupe. Please, Blaise. You're hurting me!"

He glared down her trying to figure out if she was telling the truth. He didn't release her but he loosened his grip.

She inhaled deeply. "Why are you doing this?"

"Why didn't you return my calls?"

"Because I wanted to enjoy myself for the night without your interference."

"I see...or it's quite possible you didn't call me back because you were giving away what is mine. Tell the truth. Were you with Campion?"

"Of course not!"

"Did you allow him to taste your sweet pussy? Did he get you wet like I do? Did he make you purr like a kitten?"

"You're being disgusting, Blaise. I told you the truth."

"How about I check to make sure?" With one hand still resting on her neck, he inserted his other hand into her leggings and inside her panties. His fingers grazed the light patch of hair that rested above her tight cunt. Blaise slid his middle finger along her slit. Kaia moaned.

"Hmm. You're wet, *kæreste*. Is this for me?"

She closed her eyes and bit her bottom lip. It drove him crazy with lust when she did that. He wanted to take that plump lip and suck it into his mouth but he wouldn't kiss her, just yet. He slipped two fingers into her pussy.

"Oh, yeah, this is for me. Whoever you were with tonight didn't satisfy you properly."

"I wasn't with anyone. I swear. I just needed to unwind." She gasped as he slowly eased his fingers in and out of her wetness.

"Is that so? Hmm, you've become quite the little vixen, always wanting cock. My cock, especially. And I'm going to give it to you nice and hard as a reminder not to pull the stunt you did tonight, again." He pulled his fingers out of dripping pussy and smeared her juices against her lips.

"Lick your lips, Kaia. Taste them. That's what I've done to you."

Slowly, her tongue darted out and slid along her lips. Unable to hold back any longer, he cupped her face in his palms and planted a kiss full of hunger, passion, and anger on her lips. She was the only woman who could drive him to the point of insanity and there wasn't a damn thing he could do about it.

Blaise didn't have the patience to take her to their room. He grasped the top of her leggings and ripped them down the center. He quickly did the same to her panties, leaving her pussy exposed to his hungry gaze.

"Blaise, not here. Your sister..."

"Is sound asleep."

He fumbled with his pants and released his cock. "You see what you do to me, Kaia? As I was waiting for you, I was rock hard. He missed your pussy."

"Not like this." Kaia pressed her hand on his chest.

"Yes, like this, now shut up and take it." He cupped her ass and pulled Kaia off her feet, forcing her to wrap her arms around his neck and her legs around his waist. He thrust into her with a sigh of relief. "So fucking tight, and wet for me." He murmured as he fucked her hard and fast against the door.

Kaia's only response was a whimper as she dug her fingers into his back. Her muscles clenched his shaft, sucking him in like a vacuum. It only made him go more berserk with lust. Kaia was an addiction in his blood that he simply could not get enough of.

"That's right. Take it! Take every single inch of me."

"Blaise!" she cried out burying her face against his neck.

"You better not fucking come. You don't deserve to after the stunt you pulled tonight. You come when I say you can. You are mine. This is my pussy and you are my woman and don't you fucking forget it."

He climaxed inside of her, thrusting until he'd planted every drop of his seed.

Blaise, however, wasn't finished with her. Not by a long shot.

No sooner had her feet touched the ground, Kaia found herself in Blaise's arms. He carried her up the stairs taking two at a time. She could have fought him but it was pointless. Besides, her body was such a traitor that it had gone up in flames the second he touched her.

She'd expected him to be upset when she didn't return his calls, but this was a whole other level of upset. And the really fucked up part about it was part of her was excited by his aggressiveness. She briefly wondered if something was wrong with her for feeling this way. Maybe she was a little crazy, too.

Blaise didn't put her down until they were in the bedroom. "Strip," he ordered.

"Blaise, you already got what you wanted. Let me go to bed."

"I said strip."

Kaia removed the remains of her tattered clothing as he looked on with his icy stare. When she stood before him completely naked, he licked his lips in seeming anticipation. "Absolute perfection. Now get on the bed, on your hands and knees."

"Blaise—"

"Now!"

Kaia scrambled onto the bed to do his bidding. Her body trembled as she wondered what he'd do to her next. He'd already proven to be an adventurous lover so she knew she was in store for something unexpected.

She should have been mad at him but, at the moment, she desperately wanted to have the orgasm he'd denied her downstairs. When had she become such a cum slut? Craving something she had no business wanting. She hated this man, yet wanted him at the same time.

She watched as he undressed. Blaise had a magnificent physique. He had a swimmer's body, broad shoulders, strong arms, toned chest and tight stomach. His cock jutted forward, hard, long and uncut. He reminded her of sculpture, molded by one of the masters themselves.

Blaise climbed on the bed and positioned himself behind her. She pushed her ass against him in anticipation, only for him to bring his palm crashing against her ass with a loud smack.

"Ow," she cried out. When Kaia tried to pull away, Blaise grabbed a hand full of her hair.

"Did you think you wouldn't get punished for what you've done? You've been bad so now it's time to take your punishment." He spanked her bottom again.

"It hurts," she cried.

"I know. It's going to hurt for a bit but if you take your licks like a good girl, I'm going to make you feel very good." Smack!

"Oh, God!" Tears stung her eyes. He really wasn't holding back and her ass was on fire.

After the next smack, however, he rubbed her sore bottom, soothing the pain until it was a dull throb. Just as she relaxed, he whacked the other cheek with even more force.

"Son of a bitch!" she cried out.

Without warning, he slammed his cock into her and tightened his grip on her hair. He gripped her hips and plowed into her mercilessly. "Whose pussy is this?"

When Kaia didn't answer right away, he smacked her ass again.

"Yours!"

"What's my name?"

"Blaise."

"Tell me who this pussy belongs to!" He emphasized each word with a thrust.

"This is your pussy, Blaise."

'That's right. And, don't you fucking forget it."

Blaise positioned himself with one knee on the bed and then planted his other foot on the bed, fucking her from another angle. In this position, he hit her spot just right and she crossed her eyes as bursts of pleasure hit her so hard she started speaking in tongues. "Ohmygodmygodohmygod," she cried out.

"Don't come yet."

"Please, Blaise."

He thrust into her several more times before finally grunting as he released into her yet again. "Now come!"

Kaia screamed as she let go. It was so powerful, everything went black for a moment. Unable to hold herself up any longer, she collapsed on the bed, face down.

Blaise fell to his side and pulled her against him. "Don't ever do that again, Kaia," he muttered before kissing her on top of the head.

It took several moments before Kaia came down from the high of such an intense encounter.

Again, she had to wonder what the hell was wrong with her. Why did she allow him to do these things to her and after the end of their allotted time together, would it be as easy as she thought to walk away?

The thought thoroughly depressed her. She hadn't been with Blaise that long and she'd become the very thing she promised herself that she wouldn't. A tear slid down her cheek, followed by another and then more fell unheeded.

Blaise must have felt the moisture even though she tried not to make a sound. He raised his head to look at her. "What's the matter, Kaia?"

Kaia rolled over, turning her back to him. "Everything is the matter. This arrangement is what's the matter. You're what's the matter. I'm what's the matter."

"What do you mean," he asked softly.

"This arrangement doesn't bother you in the slightest?"

"No, why should it."

"I guess it wouldn't since you don't seem to have a conscience," she scoffed.

"Believe it or not, I do have feelings, Kaia. I'm not insensitive to this situation."

She snorted in disbelief. "You could have fooled me. No matter how much I protest, you just steamroll all over me but I guess I'm the idiot who keeps letting you."

"Kaia, one of the things I admire about you is your strong-will and determination. You say I'm making you do something you don't want but you do want this. You're just too frightened to admit it."

"How can you say that? You act as if you've known me all my life, instead of just seeing me perform and deciding you wanted me. That's not normal. People don't just do that. I had a great life before you came along. I was living out my dream. I was in a relationship and I had friends. My life wasn't perfect but it was mine to decide what to do with. But then, you came barreling into my life and changed it all. Why couldn't you just let me be?"

Blaise didn't answer right away and she didn't expect him to but finally, he said. "When I was younger, it was just me and my parents. They were good people for the most part. They were deeply in love with each other. It was almost a symbiotic, co-dependent type of relationship. Whenever you saw one, the other wouldn't be far behind. They loved each other almost to the exclusion of anyone else, even their own children. Don't get me wrong, they loved me and took good care of me. I never wanted for anything but when they were together, they only had eyes for each other. Even as a child, I could see that. I was jealous of that love and one day wanted it for myself."

"As I grew older, I almost resented them because they painted a picture of obsessive love that I didn't think was possible to obtain. I didn't understand that kind of love because I never looked at anyone and felt the way my father did when he looked at my mother and vice versa. I had just started working for my father's company when Aneka came along. She was a late in life baby and she was a joy. She was probably the first person I felt a strong love for. I mean, I loved my parents but Aneka was my world. I think I paid so much attention to her because I knew my parents would give her the same offhand kind of attention they spared me when I was growing up. So anyway, as I was saying, I was working in the company and when I wasn't helping my father build his business, I was spending time with Aneka. By now, the company was starting to grow and with that newly found wealth comes attention from the opposite sex."

"I'm a red-blooded male so, of course, I loved the attention and took what was offered to me, but it became more of a charade because I grew jaded and bitter thinking the love my parents had simply didn't exist. At least not for me. And then, one day it happened. My parents were killed in a car wreck. The authorities say it was an accident but it wasn't. It was my father's partner. Let's just say he has since been taken care of but we'll leave that for another story. Anyway, my mother died instantly. Aneka was crippled and my father, he...actually would have survived albeit with a few broken bones. But when he learned of my mother's death, he died in the hospital. It was one of those unexplainable occurrences. He simply closed his eyes and didn't wake up again. He didn't want to live without my mother."

Hearing Blaise's tale, Kaia could understand why he'd have a warped idea about love but it still didn't excuse his actions. "But, what does that have to do with me?" she wondered out loud.

"Everything. With my parents gone, I had the responsibility of raising Aneka and building the business to what it is today. But in the meantime, I started to search for that love my parents had. I wanted to know if it was real or if it had all been in my head. But, the women I encountered didn't move me. You saw what Lisbeth was like. I was with her for a while because I didn't think there was any better out there. And then one day, Aneka said she wanted to go to a festival. I'd been traveling a lot so I couldn't deny her that request. Frankly, the festival was boring and I couldn't wait to leave but I didn't want to disappoint my sister. And then, we saw an American dance troupe. They were good but nothing spectacular until this phenom came on stage. She took my breath away. I think, she took everyone's breath away. I was mesmerized by her every move. I wanted to touch her to see if she was real. And as she moved across the stage, I finally understood. That's when my obsession was born."

He spoke of the matter in such a detached way that it sent chills down her spine.

"You...you fell in love with me?" she asked, scared of the answer he'd give.

"If love is thinking about the person every waking hour of the day and dreaming about them at night, then yes. If love is wanting to destroy anyone who has so much as touched that person because you want that person for your very own, then yes. If love was going to any length to have that person, then yes. If love is sitting in the dark waiting for your lover to come home because she didn't return your calls, then fuck yes. I'm in love and I'm not going to make any apologies for that, Kaia. You are mine."

Her entire body began to shake because she was certain he meant it. "Blaise, you're eventually going to have to let me go. We agreed that I'd only stay until Aneka's surgery."

"I'm aware of that, Kaia, but..."

She rolled over to face him when he didn't finish his statement. "But what?"

"I don't see why the rest of our time together has to be contentious."

"It doesn't have to be but you make it that way. You manhandle me, embarrass me in front of my friends and complete strangers and you think I should just take everything with a smile on my face."

Blaise didn't respond right away. "You're right, Kaia."

His agreement took her by surprise. "I am?"

"Yes. I realize, I have a bit of a temper and I should get a hold of it. Look, whether you want to acknowledge it or not, there's an attraction between us. Whenever we're together, it's magic. But I don't see why we can't build on that and be friends. At least, for Aneka's sake. I'd hate to upset her."

"I don't want to upset her either, Blaise. But how do you expect this friendship to happen, when you've done so much already."

"Let's wipe the slate clean and give this a chance... at least for as long as you're here."

Kaia didn't have the energy to continuously fight him so maybe a truce was in order. "Okay, Blaise. We can start over."

He smiled revealing even white teeth. "Friends?"

"Friends," she agreed hoping she wasn't making the biggest mistake of her life.

He leaned forward and pressed his lips gently to hers.

Chapter Seventeen

"This so exciting!" Aneka squealed next to Blaise.

He patted her hand indulgently and chuckled. "Calm down, precious. The show hasn't even started."

"I know. I'm so happy to see Kaia dance again. I couldn't sleep last night because I was too excited."

Blaise smiled. "Oh, so that's why you were dozing off during breakfast this morning. I guess we're going to have to go straight home after this performance and you should go straight to bed."

"No! You promised I would get to see the cast at the end of the show."

He grinned at his sister. "I'm just teasing you, precious."

"Oh, okay." She put her finger over her lips. "Shh, the show is about to begin."

The theater went dark and a spotlight shined on the stage below. It was opening night for Bodies in Motion's four-week engagement. According to Campion, tickets had sold out for most of the shows. Blaise had kept tabs on the troupe mainly to know what Kaia was up to.

He had backed off as he'd promised he would, but it didn't mean that he wasn't still tracking her. In fact the morning after their talk, she'd left her phone on the dresser. So when Kaia had gone to take a shower, he dropped the phone on the floor and stepped on it.

Blaise told her that he accidentally knocked it on the ground when he was trying to grab something off the nightstand. But when he looked for it, he accidentally walked on it.

She'd taken what he'd told her at face value because he had offered to replace it since he was the one responsible for breaking it. Kaia had actually been grateful. And just as he planned, Blaise made a trip to the cell phone store and bought her the most expensive phone sold at that location. He then headed to his security company where they implanted a chip which enabled him to always know her location.

Where most people would have felt guilty for doing something so covert, Blaise saw it as protecting something valuable to him.

The curtain went up and the audience went silent. A classical number played and a dancer twirled onto the stage. It was Patty. She whirled around and jumped and kicked. Blaise didn't know a lot about dance beside what Kaia had told him but he could tell the redhead was quite good. Then another dancer came on stage followed by another. Soon the stage was filled with all the dancers in the troupe. Kaia came out last. She twirled to the center and all of the dancers did a synchronized number, moving as one. But Blaise only had eyes for Kaia.

Though he was biased when it came to her, it was clear she was the best dancer in her group. It was no wonder she was the star of the show.

Aneka leaned over and whispered. "Kaia dances like an angel."

"That she does. That she does," Blaise answered back, his eyes never leaving the stage.

When the number was over, the audience applauded. Kaia, however, was not in the next two numbers and Blaise found himself shifting in his seat impatiently. At least his sister was still entertained.

Finally, when Kaia appeared on the stage again, she was in a shimmering white dress that sparkled on her body like diamonds. She was so beautiful, she literally took his breath away. He gripped his armrests to stop himself from getting out of his seat and going down to the stage. He wanted her all to himself but he couldn't rob her of this moment when he knew it meant so much to her.

The way she moved her body so sensually had his dick at attention. Blaise was enraptured as was the rest of the audience. The way she glided across the stage was a thing of beauty. She leaped into the air and did a full split followed by a series of twirls. It was a wonder how she didn't get dizzy. She was as graceful as a swan. According to the program, it was ironically named, the swan dance. Kaia did a series of acrobatic moves. When she went into a backflip without any hands, Aneka grabbed his hand. "*Fantastiske!*"

Blaise could only nod, his eyes never leaving the stage. At the end of the routine, she went down to her knees and placed her hands and forehead against the floor. She remained in that position for a while. But then the music changed and Campion came prancing on stage.

Blaise had to grip the armrests yet again. He hated that little shit. But he had to admit the other man had talent. Nothing compared to Kaia's talent in his opinion but Campion was still good. He danced around Kaia until she gracefully stood up again, like an awakening.

They danced together so intimately. The way their faces conveyed emotion one would think they were still together. Campion lifted Kaia several times and spun her around. She contorted around her dance partner in a way that almost seemed unreal.

When the number ended. The crowd was on their feet. Blaise remained seated out of deference to Aneka, but he didn't know if he could move even if he wanted to. Seeing Kaia dance again had been a gift. It was what she was born to do.

Kaia was in two more numbers but in each routine, she managed to outshine everyone on stage. Even for someone so compact, her presence when she danced was larger than life. The show ended with thunderous applause.

He could watch Kaia dance over and over again.

Blaise waited for the crowd to thin before wheeling Aneka to the elevator and then to the backstage area where he had access. When he made his way to where the dressing rooms were, there were dancers gathered in the hallway, congratulating themselves and talking with well-wishers.

A few of the dancers acknowledged him and politely came to speak to Aneka who seemed to be in her element. His sister told the dancers how much she enjoyed the show and asked lots of questions that thankfully they all answered patiently.

Obsessed

Blaise was grateful that they were nice to Aneka but he was certain that it didn't hurt that she was related to the show's biggest backer. It wasn't that his sweet sister wasn't charming in her own right. It was simply the fact that he knew how the world worked. Impatient to find Kaia, he wheeled Aneka's chair further down the hall and found Kaia surrounded by a handful of adoring fans who were fortunate enough to get backstage access.

When she saw him, she smiled. She was absolutely beautiful. She practically glowed as she was probably still on a high from her performance. His heart flipped in his chest, seeing that she'd smiled just for him. He wanted to take her in his arms and fuck her until the only word she could utter was his name.

Ever since they'd had their talk things had been more cordial between them. Kaia had started to open up to him about her life. She talked about dance a lot and how it had helped her get through the most difficult times in her life. She briefly talked about her mother who had also been a dancer. It was clear Kaia still grieved for her mother after all this time.

Although he already had an extensive file on her, it was nice getting to know her up close and in person. He learned that she didn't eat red meat and her favorite food was sushi and she had a weakness for salt and vinegar potato chips. When she wasn't dancing she kept in shape by running and weight training. She loved dogs but was too busy to have a pet.

Blaise loved the friendship that Kaia had with his sister. It was clear that Aneka hero-worshiped Kaia. Blaise knew that his sister could be a chatterbox whenever she was excited about something to the point where he'd often have to tell her not to talk so much. But to Kaia's credit, she was always patient with the preteen. Blaise could tell Kaia was great with children in general. He'd happened to observe her hip hop dance class at the recreation center she volunteered at and those children adored her.

And their children would adore Kaia as well. The very thought of her heavy with his child, made his cock stir. Blaise took a few calming breaths to get his body under control as he approached her.

Kaia leaned over and gave Aneka a hug. "Did you guys enjoy the show?"

"It was the best thing I've ever seen in my life. I loved everything about it. The swan dance was my favorite. You were so beautiful," Aneka gushed.

Kaia chuckled. "Aww, thank you, sweetie. I'm glad you enjoyed it." She raised her head and looked at Blaise. "And how about you?"

"Well, you already know how I feel without even asking."

"I mean about the show."

"I only noticed you, but I suppose the rest of the show was acceptable."

Her eyes darted away from his as she let out a nervous titter. "I'm sure you must have an opinion on the other performances that weren't mine."

Blaise sighed. "Yes, they were entertaining but again, you were the only one I really paid attention to. When you weren't on stage, I was simply biding my time."

Kaia bit her bottom lip. "Well, I'm glad you enjoyed my number. And I wanted to thank you for that large bouquet you had sent to my dressing room. I don't think I've ever received an arrangement so grand. Five dozen roses seems a bit over the top. How am I going to get them all home?" she laughed.

Blaise shrugged. "Give them away if you'd like. They're simply a symbol of my admiration for you. Besides, there are more roses when we get home."

"Blaise, what did you do? Buy out a florist?"

"Something like that."

"Would you mind very much if I can talk to some of the other dancers?" Aneka interrupted.

"Of course, precious. Give me a moment," Blaise answered before returning his attention to Kaia. "So will you be going home with us?"

"Well, actually a bunch of us usually go out to eat to celebrate opening night and I'd really like to go."

Blaise flexed the muscle in his jaw. His first instinct was to tell her hell no, but now that he could track her every move, he'd at least know where she was. He took a deep breath. "Of course. I wouldn't begrudge you time with your colleagues, although I trust you won't be out too late?"

"Of course not. After tonight's performance, I might be too exhausted for much else."

He took her by the wrist and pulled her against him, giving her a long deep kiss on the lips. "Something to remember me by." He said before wheeling his sister away.

Kaia touched her lips as she watched Blaise's retreating back. She knew why he'd kissed her. To stake his claim but she'd done nothing to stop him. She noticed several curious stares in her direction, a few of them were hostile. One of them was Landon's but she could care less what he thought. He was the one who'd practically pushed her into Blaise's arms, so he had no right to be upset.

Her relationship with Blaise, if one could call it that, was changing and she couldn't quite put her finger on how or why. Sure he was still a brute who seemed to stop at nothing to get his way but since their talk. He'd calmed down considerably. He was actually quite pleasant to be around.

One of the things she liked about Blaise was his relationship with Aneka. It was clear that he loved that little girl to distraction, spoiling her shamelessly but he was still firm with her when it was necessary. He would make a good father one day with whomever he finally settled down with. But that woman couldn't be her. She also learned that Blaise actually had a sense of humor. His deadpan delivery often made her giggle. Then there were the down times they spent together at night after Aneka and her nurse had gone to bed.

It wasn't simply the sex which was still something quite out of the ordinary, they would talk afterward and Blaise revealed bits and pieces about his life. It fascinated her to learn that this man who was only thirty-four had built upon his father's legacy to make his company what it was today. But there was a ruthless streak about him that she found a little frightening. For instance, when he'd briefly mentioned his father's old business partner, Blaise didn't explicitly say that he'd done something to the man but it was the way he'd said the situation had been 'handled', told her far more than she wanted to know. Blaise Lundgaard was a conundrum she was still trying to figure out.

This thing that they had, though ever-evolving couldn't last. Blaise was much too intense for her. He would end up smothering her and after having her eyes opened up to the kind of man Landon was she couldn't be with someone who would willing to walk all over her dreams for their own means.

But even as this thought occurred to Kaia, she felt a little sad about the thought of walking away in a few months. Again, she had to ask herself what was wrong with her? She should be finding ways to resist this man at every chance she got, but every day she found herself falling further under his spell.

Kaia was jolted out of her thoughts when someone bumped into her, nearly knocking her off her feet. "Hey!" she called out when she noticed who the perpetrator was

"Oops. I didn't see you there." Deena placed her hand over her mouth in a parody of shock.

Kaia glared at her rival. Tonight wasn't the time nor place to cause a scene, especially with people from outside of the company surrounding them, but apparently, the brunette had been spoiling for a fight for days. The last several days of rehearsal, Deena would make rude comments to Kaia, loud enough for her to hear. Deena would complain loudly about Kaia receiving special favors. She'd basically gone out of her way to make Kaia miserable. Kaia however, had done her best to ignore the other woman but she'd had enough. "Aren't you tired of being such a bitch all the time?"

"And aren't you tired of sucking dick to get ahead?" Deena sneered.

Kaia was so over this woman. "Deena, you're a talented dancer, but you are a rotten human being. Instead of worrying about what I'm doing all time and who's dick I'm sucking, perhaps you should focus on yourself. The truth is, you're so jealous of me that you can't see straight so you say nasty things to make yourself feel better. But we both know that I'm better than you on my worst day than you are at your best. And the only reason why I haven't shoved my foot up your ass yet is because you're a pathetic wannabe who will never be me. So kick rocks, and stay out of my way." She walked past Deena making sure she returned the favor by bumping into her.

Kaia headed to her dressing room and was hit by the overwhelming scent of the roses. The arrangement was spread throughout the entire room. Patty was inside changing because she shared the room with three other dancers.

"I swear I'm going to end up smelling like roses, before I leave this place," Patty joked.

"It is a bit overwhelming," Kaia sighed as she grabbed an outfit off the hook to change into.

"But it's a sweet gesture. I know it was kind of heavy-handed the way Blaise went after you but it's clear that the man is quite smitten with you. I saw the way he was looking at you."

"I know. I don't know what to make of it sometimes. It's like part of me knows that this arrangement we have is wrong but... I don't know. He's kind of growing on me. You don't think it's Stockholm Syndrome or something like that, do you?"

"I don't know what to tell you but if I had a wealthy man who looked as sexy as Blaise Lundgaard, I wouldn't be putting up much of a fight."

"Come on Patty, be serious. We both know what he did was pretty fucked up. But the more time I spend with him, it's not so bad. Does that make me crazy?"

Patty seemed to contemplate this for a moment. "I don't think so. I believe that humans are so resilient because of the way we fight for survival. We all have coping mechanisms and yours is your eternal optimism. You're always looking at the bright side of things. And I've already told you that if you weren't such a nice person, I'd hate your guts because you're the total package, pretty and talented and genuine. So I don't think you're crazy. I just think you're coping. And maybe it is a bit crazy all the things Blaise did to get you but...even I have to admit the guy seems to be really into you."

But what Kaia couldn't figure out: was it just intense feelings or an unhealthy obsession?

"Anyway, I saw you having words with Deena. I swear she isn't satisfied unless she's causing drama."

Kaia shrugged, not wanting to get into it. She wouldn't let the other woman ruin was an otherwise amazing night. "It was just Deena being Deena. It's not even worth talking about her." Kaia grabbed a towel to hit the showers.

"Well, you're a better person than me because I would have yanked her hair out of her roots a long time ago if I was you. You know her and Landon had been hanging out a lot, recently."

For some reason, that news didn't bother her as much as it probably should have but Kaia just shrugged it off. "Those two deserve each other."

Just then there was a knock on her door. "Come in," she answered.

Landon poked his head in the door. "There's a gentleman outside who said he wanted to speak with you. He said it was quite urgent. Maybe it's another one of your admirers," Landon threw in that low blow and Kaia wanted to throw something at his head.

Holding back her angry retort she replied calmly, "He didn't say who he was?"

"No."

"You didn't ask?"

"I can't keep track of all the men chasing after you."

"You really are an ass, Landon. I don't know what I ever saw in you."

"Probably a means to an end," he said before closing the door.

"Asshole!" Patty shouted.

"Forget about him, he's not worth it."

"Girl, if you need someone to help you stomp a mud hole in his ass then I have you back."

Kaia laughed. "Duly noted. I really need to take a shower before everyone uses up the hot water, but I guess I should go out there to see who it is."

"Probably one of your adoring fans," Patty teased dramatically.

Kaia giggled as she headed to the door. "If you want to take some of these flowers home, you're welcome to them. There's no way I'm going to be able to get them home on my own."

"Well, I don't mind if I do. This way I can pretend I have an adoring fan."

Kaia was still smiling when she went outside to see who her mysterious visitor was. Landon pointed to a man who had his back to her. When he turned around, however, the smile instantly fell from Kaia's face.

"Kaia, it's good to see you," the older gentleman stepped forward.

"Daddy?"

Chapter Eighteen

Kaia was still in shock as she sat down in front of the man she hadn't seen in years. It was like seeing a ghost. The last person in the world she'd expected to come see her was her father who she hadn't seen since he'd walked out on her and her mother without a backward glance. Most of her life she told herself that she was better off without him, after all, what kind of man would just up and leave his family? Divorce was one thing but you simply didn't abandon your children.

All the old hurt she thought she'd buried a long time ago, resurfaced. Her first instinct was to tell him to go to hell. Her second was to ask him where the hell he'd been after all these years.

After she had gotten her emotions under control, Kaia asked him what he wanted.

Darren Benson had shifted uncomfortably on his feet and asked if he could take her out for a meal so that they could talk. Kaia wanted to refuse but then she realized she might never get another opportunity to ask him the questions that had haunted her for years.

After a quick shower, she dressed, gathered her belongings and they ended up going to a seafood restaurant down the street. Kaia couldn't stop staring at her father. He looked almost exactly like he did years ago except for the liberal sprinkles of gray in his otherwise dark head of hair.

"You can order whatever you like. My treat," Darren said as Kaia perused through the menu.

"Gee, how generous of you," Kaia responded not bothering to keep the sarcasm from her voice.

Darren was a dark-skinned man, but he blanched under Kaia's unwavering scrutiny. She had nothing to be ashamed of. He was the one who left her. He hadn't even reached out to her when her mother had died.

As she thought about that, the resentment came flooding back. "Why did you come to my show anyway? Why now after all this time? You walked out on mom and me thirteen years ago."

"Those are fair questions and I'll answer them as best as I can. Do you want to order your meal first?"

Kaia was hungry, she usually was after a performance but food wasn't her priority at the moment. She thought about how much she cried when her father had left. She remembered that day clearly. She'd come home from school and her mother was sitting at the kitchen table with tears streaming down her face. And then Kaia noticed suitcases at the door.

"What's going on Mama?"

"He's leaving us."

"Who?"

"Your father. He's leaving us for someone else."

Obsessed

Just then her father walked into the kitchen. "Don't tell her that, Cynthia. You know that isn't the reason."

"Don't bother lying now. You got some other whore pregnant and now you're leaving your family to set up house with her and your little bastard."

Kaia had a pretty active imagination but she wasn't exactly sure what her mother meant by all of that. All she knew was that her mother was upset and her father looked very guilty like the time she'd been caught after staying up late to watch an R rated movie.

"Do not say that about her. I never meant for things to be like this, but you know things haven't been right with us for a long time."

"Then go and be with your bitch!" her mother screamed.

Darren just shook his head and looked at Kaia. "Baby, I'm so sorry you have to see this. I'll be in touch. I promise." He gave her a brief hug and with that, he walked out of the door and out of her life.

That was the last time she'd seen him until right now.

"No, I want the answers I believe I deserve and then we can part ways and never see each other again."

Darren sighed. "I understand why you wouldn't want to see me and I thought long and hard about this, wondering if there would ever be a right time to reach out to you. But I was in New York for business and I saw a poster for your dance company on a building. I recognized you right away. So I bought tickets to this show and there you were, my beautiful princess. I just wanted to tell you that I'm so proud of you and I'm glad to see you pursuing your dreams. Your mother would have been proud."

"You don't get to mention my mother, ever."

Darren sighed. "It's not my intention to upset you, Kaia. It's just...whether you believe it or not, I miss you and I was hoping we could just talk and maybe iron out our differences."

"What differences? You left Mom and me without a backward glance. And now you just waltz back into my life and expect everything to be okay? It doesn't work like that, Darren. And unless you start answering questions, I'm going to get up and walk away."

He nodded. "You're right. I was just thinking about myself. I can imagine this isn't easy for you to have this confrontation."

Just then the waitress returned to the table to take their orders. Her father ordered a steak while Kaia ordered the grilled sea bass with a side salad. Once the waitress walked away Kaia returned her attention back to her father. "Well, why? I just need to know why you are here after all this time."

"Because I think it's time to right some wrongs. Look, your mother and I weren't happy together. We weren't happy for a long time, actually. I'm not placing the blame on anyone but we were young when we met. She was this beautiful dancer with so many hopes and dreams and of course I fell for her, at least what I believed love to be. We fell for each other. It was all fun and games with us for a while but then we realized we didn't have a whole lot in common outside of the bedroom. Pardon me for being so graphic."

"I'm an adult."

"Yes, you are. A very accomplished one. You went Julliard. That's a pretty big deal."

She wasn't sure how he knew that but Kaia wasn't the least bit moved.

"Please get to the point."

"I'm sorry. I'm rambling. I guess I'm nervous. After all, I didn't think you'd actually want to see me."

"Well, I'm here so you might as well, get off your chest what you need to, otherwise we should end this pointless meeting."

"It's not pointless to me." He took a sip from his water glass. "Well, your mother and I were on the verge of splitting up when she found out she was pregnant. I wanted to do the right thing so I asked her to marry me. We wanted to make things work for your sake. And for a while we did. I don't think anyone would call what we had a picturesque love but we did our best to make it work until it didn't."

"But we had fought hard to stay together because we didn't want to break up the family. We wanted you to have a stable home life but we continued to drift apart and the arguments became bigger than either one of us could fix. They were really bad. They'd progressed from yelling to throwing things. The situation got out of hand. The problem was, we were trying to hold on to something that had died a long time ago. It was so stressful at home that I started staying out late and sometimes I avoided coming home altogether. That's when I met Wendy."

"I admit, I was wrong for pursuing something I had no business to but she listened to my problems and it nice being with someone who seemed to understand me. In Wendy's defense, I didn't tell her that I was married, so when she found out she left me. I decided to give things one more try with your mother but Wendy came to me to let me know that she was pregnant and I realized that I loved her and I couldn't remain in a situation that made everyone so unhappy. I wish I would have done things differently but there you have it. That's why I left."

Kaia wanted to feel sympathetic toward his plight but she couldn't muster the fucks to give. He'd cheated and got another woman pregnant behind her mother's back and that was supposed to be okay. But on the other hand she was mature enough to realize that relationships didn't always work out and sometimes it was better to be apart for one's peace of mind. But Kaia also remembered the nights her mother used to cry herself to sleep. Those were the nights when Kaia would curl up in bed next to her mother and they'd fall asleep holding on to each other. Eventually, her mother moved on with her life, but Kai could tell that Cynthia never quite got over her ex's betrayal.

"I'm not sure what you want me to say about that? You divorce spouses, not your children. Was it that easy for you to walk away from me as well?"

The waitress brought out their food cutting off anything her father would have said in response. When they were alone again, Kaia took a bite of her food. She was sure it was delicious, it certainly looked appetizing but she couldn't taste a thing.

After a few more bites, she pushed her plate away.

"Is the food not to your liking?"

"I'm not hungry anymore."

"No? I would think you'd have a big appetite after all that dancing."

"So you're just going to sit there and pretend like this is some happy father-daughter reunion? It's not. You have yet to explain why you never came to see me. It's not like you didn't know where we were. We stayed in the same house."

"You're right and that was on me but I did try. I promise you I did. I sent emails but you never responded. I sent letters the old fashioned way and they were all returned unopened. I tried to call you but your mother said you didn't want to talk to me. I even came to the house to visit but you would never be there. After a while, I got the hint. I figured you'd speak to me when you were ready. But then as the time lapsed, it just got hard to reach out to you."

Kaia shook her head in disgust. "You're a liar. I never got a single email or letter from you. And my mother would have told me if you called."

"Your mother was still very upset with me for leaving."

"Don't you dare! You don't get to leave and start a whole new family and then slander my mom when she's not here to defend herself. You know what? Fuck this. I knew it was a mistake coming here with you."

"I'm not trying to make your mom look bad and I'm sure she probably had her reasons for doing what she did. But it's the truth."

"Well, you obviously didn't try hard enough. You could have gone to court to petition for visitation rights."

His eyes darted away from hers. "You're right. There are things I could have done differently. I guess I figured when you were ready you'd come to me. But I thought about you over the years. You have two little sisters by the way. One of them actually wants to be a dancer. If she turns out to half as good as you, I know she'll succeed."

A resentment she didn't expect reared its head. She pushed away from the table and stood up. "Well, I hope you are a better father to them than you were to. This was a pointless exercise."

Darren caught her wrist when she tried to leave. "Please don't go. I just want to get to know you again."

"Well, it's too late for that. I don't want anything to do with you." Kaia attempted to pull away but he held firm.

"At the very least take my card in case you want to get in contact with me. Please. I'd love for you to meet your sisters."

"Oh yeah, and what about your wife?"

"She knows about you and is supportive of us forging a relationship."

"It's too bad she wasn't so supportive sooner."

"Just take my card, okay?"

Kaia snatched her card out of his hand so that he could let her go. "Are you done?"

He bowed his head in defeat and released her wrist. "Yes, Kaia no matter what you think, I never stopped caring about you. You're my little girl and nothing will change that."

"If it helps you to sleep at night to think that then go for it. Goodbye."

She stormed out of the restaurant with tears swimming in her eyes.

"Kaia," someone called her name.

She looked up to see Blaise standing by a slick silver sports car. "Blaise, what are you doing here? How did you know I'd be here?"

As far as she knew he didn't know she would be having dinner with her father. She didn't even know until a couple hours ago.

"After I took Aneka out for ice cream, she fell asleep in the car, so I took her back home and decided to join you and the rest of your troupe. As the largest backer, I was invited."

"Oh, I don't remember telling you where it was."

"I'm still in touch with Campion. Anyway, when I went to the restaurant you were supposed to be at you obviously weren't there. Someone mentioned you saying you were heading here instead."

Kaia frowned. She didn't remember telling anyone about her plans to dine with her father but in her highly emotional state, she might have mentioned something to Patty.

She eyed the sporty vehicle. "This is your car?"

"Yes, get in."

He opened the passenger door for her. "Honestly, I didn't know that you could drive. You usually have a driver chauffeur you everywhere."

"Yes, I drive, and I drive quite well."

"Blaise, do you mind if we just drive around the city for a while. I don't really feel like going back to the penthouse."

"Of course. Your wish is my command."

Eve Vaughn

Chapter Nineteen

Blaise was anxious to find Kaia when he realized that she didn't go to dinner with the rest of the dancers. So he went looking for her. She didn't need to know that he found her through the tracker on her phone. He had every intention of dragging her out of the restaurant with whoever she was with but just as he was about to hand his keys to the valet, Kaia came running out of the restaurant and it was clear that she was distraught.

If he learned nothing, he found that he made more progress with Kaia when he took a more laid-back approach. As long as she believed she was in control of the situation he could bend things to his will more easily.

That Kaia didn't want to go home, played into his hands because he could question her casually and make it look completely natural. Kaia didn't say anything and neither did he for several minutes. The only sound in his vehicle was the radio playing on low.

"You seem upset about something, Kaia. Do you want to talk about it?" he asked trying to stay as calm as possible.'

She didn't answer right away.

Blaise took one hand off the steering wheel to place it on her thigh. "Do you remember what we talked about? About us being friends. I may be your lover, Kaia, but I want you to be able to tell me when something is bothering you."

"I had intended to go to dinner with the rest of the crew but I got an unexpected visitor."

She spoke so low, he almost had to strain to hear her. He pressed the button on the center of the steering wheel to turn off the radio. "Who was it?"

"My father."

"Your father?" This even surprised him. As far as Blaise knew, Darren Benson was living happily with his wife and two children. What was he doing in New York? He would be sure to look into it tomorrow.

"So it was him you were having dinner with? Was he alone?"

"Yes."

"I can tell from the way you came storming out of the restaurant it wasn't a happy reunion."

"No, I wouldn't call it that. It turned pretty ugly real fast. I didn't even want to go out with him at first. I mean I haven't seen him since I was ten. And now 13 years later he's decided he wants to be in my life. I'm kind of suspicious of his motives. Maybe he only wants to see me now because he needs a kidney or something."

"Hmm. Or perhaps he genuinely wants to get to know you better. Has that thought occurred to you?"

"I might have actually believed him if he didn't try to make himself look better at the expense of my mother. After he left things were hard for us. My mother scrimped and saved because he'd simply abandoned us. He told me that he tried to contact me but I never received any calls, letters or emails. He even said he tried to visit me but my mother wouldn't let him speak to me. My mother wouldn't have done that to me."

Blaise contemplated what she'd just said before replying. "You said that your mother struggled after he left? Did you have to move after the divorce?"

Kaia frowned. "No, but I don't understand what that has to do with anything."

"Well, since he just abandoned you without any kind of support, it must have been hard to keep up with the bills."

"She had to take a couple of part-time jobs to make ends meet."

"I see." From the file that Blaise had of her family history, he knew for a fact that Darren Benson had paid child support for Kaia up until she was eighteen. That Kaia didn't know this seemed strange. Perhaps her father was telling the truth. It wouldn't have been the first time that a scorned partner used their child to exact revenge against their ex-partner. But disclosing this information to Kaia wouldn't benefit him seeing how she idolized her mother.

Besides, in this vulnerable state, she was opening up to him in ways she never had before.

"So I take it that you have no plan to reach out to him again."

She shook her head. "No. Blaise, you have no idea what I went through when I was a child. I cried every night for months because all I wanted was my daddy. And what made matters worse, my mom was completely broken when he walked out on us. I felt so left out during father-daughter dances and I missed the little things he used to do with me. I would lie awake at night wondering what was wrong with me that my own father didn't want me. How could a man walk away from his kid so easily? I wondered if he thought about me and if he did, why didn't he come for me?" A tear slid down her cheek.

Blaise briefly took his eyes off the road to wipe the stray tear away with his thumb. "I'm sorry you feel that way. But I want you to know that there is absolutely nothing wrong with you, *kæreste*. You are perfect in every way. His abandonment was his fault. Not yours, so never doubt yourself again."

She sniffed with a nod. "Thanks, Blaise. Intellectually, I know it wasn't my fault but it still wreaks havoc on my self-esteem. To this day, I feel a little twinge in my heart when I see fathers and daughters together. Even seeing you and Aneka together, does something to me. I know you're her brother, but you're like a father to her. And now to hear that he has two other daughters he's raising. I mean, I have two sisters I knew nothing about. It's kind of fucked up that I'm jealous of a couple kids who probably don't know that their father is a deadbeat."

Her confession explained so much. Blaise often wondered what it was that made such a vibrant, talented woman so insecure. She was brilliant at what she did and she quite lovely but often she doubted herself. That was probably how she'd ended up with an opportunist like Campion in the first place. He'd exploited Kaia's vulnerability to his advantage. Blaise knew he wasn't much better than Campion in some respects but all was fair in love and war. And he played for keeps.

"What if your sisters eventually want to have a relationship with you, Kaia? Would you turn them away?"

She shrugged. "I don't know. Like I said before, it's not their fault who their father is. But if I welcome them into my life that would also mean having my father close by and his *wife.*" Kaia practically spit the word wife out as if she found it to be particularly distasteful.

"That's understandable."

Silence settled over them once more. Blaise continued to drive and they took in the city lights.

"Blaise, let's go somewhere. To a club. I want to dance and let loose."

"A club? As in one of those places with loud music and people packed together like sardines? That's not exactly my idea of a good time."

Kaia placed her hand on his thigh. "Please?"

"Fine, but I'll pick a spot. I'll call one of my friends who owns a few clubs around the city who can get us in."

Blaise pushed the blue tooth button on the car's console and instructed it to call his friend.

Within a few minutes, their names were on the VIP list for one a club downtown called The Fish Tank.

"I can't believe we're going to The Fish Tank. That's one of the hottest clubs in the city. I've been there once but they wouldn't let everyone in."

"Oh, why is that?"

"Well, it was a handful of us. They were only going to let the girls in but not the guys. The said there were too many men in the club already. So if all of us couldn't get in, I said forget it."

"That's one of the reasons why you're so special Kaia."

She raised a brow. "Why is that?"

"Because you care about other people. I know plenty of men and women who would have gone into that club and not thought twice about leaving their friends behind."

She shrugged. "That's not my style. Besides, that's just common human decency."

If he was a decent human being he would set her free but he was in too deep. He would hold on to this woman with everything he had and would make no apologies for it.

When they pulled up to the club, Blaise helped Kaia out of his car. Surprisingly, she felt better after talking to him. But Kaia wanted to put the conversation she had with her father behind her and just toss all her worries away. She didn't want to think about Darren Benson or the tense interaction she'd had with Deena earlier. She wanted to put all her troubles behind her and just feel but happy for once.

Blaise gave his name to the bouncer and they were allowed right her. The club was decorated in blue neon and gold light. It felt like being in a large fishbowl. Blaise took her hand and led her upstairs to one of the private VIP rooms where they could see everyone from blown and still hear the music.

Their room had chilled champagne waiting for them. "This is for us?"

"Yes, my friend arranged it. One of the privileges of having connections."

"I'll say."

"Shall I pour you a glass?" He held the champagne bottle up.

"Yes, please." Even though she wasn't much of a drinker she wanted to feel as numb as possible.

Blaise uncorked the bottle and poured two glasses. "Here's to us," he toasted.

"To us." She held up her glass and clinked it against his.

The bubbles tickled her nose as she drank it. "Mmm, this is delicious."

"It should be, these bottles are a thousand dollars a pop," he said as if he was talking about pocket change.

Kaia nearly spit her champagne out. "That's a lot."

He held his glass up to her and winked. "I'm not complaining. Drink and enjoy Kaia. This is what you wanted."

He had a point. Seeing no point in wasting the drink, she asked for another glass. By the third, she could feel the effects kicking in. She danced around the room gyrating to the rhythm. Her body was warm and tingling as the alcohol worked through her system.

Blaise watched silently as she danced. Maybe it was the champagne that lowered her inhibition or maybe because she simply didn't give a damn at the moment, she closed the distance between her and Blaise and started to move her body against his. She ran her hands down his body and dropped low to the ground before shimmying her way up his body. She then turned around and grinded her ass into his pelvis. She felt his erection poke her.

Blaise wrapped his hand around her neck and pulled her close to him. "Don't start something you can't finish, *kæreste*."

Her only response was to smile.

Blaise groaned as she continued to wiggle her bottom against his dick. For some reason, she was incredibly horny and she wanted to feel good.

Blaise captured her earlobe in his teeth and gave it a little nip making her gasp. He then cupped her breast in his palm as she continued to wiggle against him. She was, fortunately, wearing a dress tonight which gave Blaise easy access to her pussy. With one hand still resting on her breast, he slid the other one up her dressed rubbing her thigh up and down. He then went higher, not stopping until he reached her panties.

"Part your legs for me."

Kaia did as she was told, arching her back against him. She raised her arm to hook around his neck as he pushed the crotch of her panties aside and eased a finger inside of her.

"You're so wet for me. You want it bad tonight, don't you?"

"Yes," she moaned riding his finger.

Kaia didn't want to think. She'd worry about this tomorrow but until then nothing else mattered.

Blaise fingered her while twisting her nipples through her dress. She was so turned on she couldn't keep still. "More," she demanded needed to be filled by him.

He pushed another finger into her. "All this passion, just for me," he groaned, working her body like a fine-tuned instrument.

She was so turned on his fingers simply weren't enough, she needed him inside of her.

Kaia grabbed his wrist and pulled his hand away from her body. She twisted around until she was facing him. "I need you now." She pointed to the couch. "Sit."

Blaise raised his brow in apparent surprise. "So you're in charge now?"

"Absolutely. Now park your ass over there." She shoved him by the shoulders, guiding him to the couch.

Blaise took a seat with his legs spread. Kaia went to her knees and unbuckled his pants. She reached into his briefs and pulled out his shaft. It was thick and long. The mushroom-shaped tip, poked out from the foreskin. Wrapping her hand around his member, she lowered her head and took it into her mouth.

"Shit!" he grunted.

Kaia took as much of him as she could into her mouth. When it hit the back of her throat she slid her head up and down, working him with her hand as she went.

Blaise grabbed a handful of her hair and guided her along his shaft. "So fucking good. That's it *kæreste*, suck it good."

She got him nice and wet as she dragged her tongue along his length. It turned her on to know that she could do this to him and drive him to this point of need.

Kaia would have kept going but Blaise pulled her up by the shoulders.

"Get on this dick. Now!"

Kaia stood up and put pushed her panties down her hips and kicked them off. She then straddled him and grabbed his cock.

"That's right, put it in you."

She slowly lowered herself on him and sighed from the sensation of being deliciously stretched. She placed her hands on his shoulders to brace herself. Blaise grasped her hips as she moved up and up down. It took her a few strokes to find her rhythm but when she did, she bounced up and down on his dick in an erotic dance that was created just for them. She clenched her muscles around him.

Blaise grunted as he raised his hips each time she lowered her pussy on him.

"All mine. I'll never let you go," he promised.

His words didn't quite register because she was too lost in the moment. She didn't want this to end.

If anyone would have told her that she would end up having sex in a nightclub of all places, she would have laughed in their face. Yet here she was and loving every second of it. Blaise had opened her up to things Kaia never thought she'd ever experience.

Her orgasm hit her hard and fast, swiftly moving through her body like a tidal wave.

Blaise dug his fingers into her hips and shot his seed deep in inside of her. He pressed his lips against hers and whispered. "Let's go home."

Chapter Twenty

It was the last night of their run before Bodies in Motion took another break and frankly it couldn't have come soon enough. Tensions were running high among the dancers and it didn't help matters that Landon and Deena were stoking the flames. Landon had become increasingly hostile toward Kaia, finding fault in everything she did even though Kaia executed her moves perfectly. Deena who had been feeding off of Landon's negative energy continued to spread rumors about Kaia although the brunette was never stupid enough to come to Kaia with that bullshit.

It finally came to a point where she was only talking to her core friends because everyone was so divided. The only upside was actually performing. The show was such a success that Landon hinted at upcoming opportunities. He mentioned that he had a major announcement after this show and everyone was on edge.

Kaia wasn't feeling well. In fact, she hadn't been feeling well for the past several days. She wasn't sure if she was coming down with something but she constantly felt as if she had to throw up.

Maybe it was the stress of Landon acting like a complete douche. Or it could have been that Aneka's surgery was the following week, and that would end her time with Blaise.

These past several weeks had been unexpected. She and Blaise had actually formed a tight friendship. She would share things about her life that she hadn't told many people and he would always listen and never judged. He was still on the possessive side but she'd gotten used to it. And the lovemaking—sex was an addiction that she couldn't shake.

It made her uneasy that he would refer to what they did as lovemaking when there was no love involved. She told herself that she didn't love him but Kaia found Blaise slowly creeping into her thoughts. Whenever she had a particularly rough day he would do something for her like make sure the cook made her favorite meal or he'd take her and Aneka to someplace special to cheer her up. She was actually happy to see him whenever he came home.

She's tried hard to deny it but she was actually developing feelings for Blaise, but how could anything come of it when their agreement was over. If Aneka's surgery was a success, they'd be heading back to Demark and she would stay in the states and dance. A few months ago that would have filled her with relief. Now all she felt was dread. She would miss Aneka who had become a dear friend to her. And as for Blaise...she'd especially miss him. Did that make her as crazy as he was for falling for someone who'd strong-armed his way into her life? She wasn't sure what was wrong with her.

Kaia laid on the couch of her dressing room trying to get over the nauseous feeling torturing her stomach. She'd taken an antacid but it wasn't working.

Miranda, Patty, and Jackie chatted on the other side of the room. Kaia wasn't really paying attention to the conversation until Patty called her name to get her attention.

"Hey, Kaia. Are you going to be all right? You don't look so hot."

"I don't know. I think I may be getting a bug or something."

Patty eyed her thoughtfully. "Are you sure you're going to be able to go on?"

"Yes, I'm sure when I get on stage, I'll be just fine." Just as the words left her mouth, Kaia sprang to her feet and rushed to the bathroom. She threw up the contents of her stomach which was a light lunch she'd had a few hours ago."

Patty walked into the bathroom with concern etched on her face. "Are you sure you're okay?"

Kaia hugged the toilet bowl feeling slightly better now that her stomach was empty. "Yes. Maybe I had something that didn't agree with me."

"Or maybe you could be pregnant."

Kaia stiffened. "That's not possible. I've taken my birth control faithfully."

"The only birth control that's 100 percent is abstinence and something tells me there is nothing chaste about your relationship with Blaise."

Though it wasn't likely, it scared the shit out of Kaia at the thought of being pregnant. What would Blaise say? He'd probably think she was trying to trap him.

She couldn't have a baby now. She had a thriving career she didn't want to give up. She was twenty-three and unmarried and whatever she had with Blaise was still a mystery to her.

"No. Absolutely not." She shook her head vehemently. "I'm not pregnant."

"Well, the sure way of finding out is to take a pregnancy test."

"No. I'm not pregnant and I'm not going to talk about this anymore."

Patty shrugged. "Suit yourself."

Kaia didn't mean to snap at her friend who she knew was only trying to help. "I'm sorry Patty. I guess I'm just a bit on edge with the way things have been these past few weeks."

"Yeah, Landon has turned into a major asswipe. But don't let that twerp get under your skin. We're going to kill tonight's performance."

Kaia smiled for the first time that night.

By the time she got on stage, later on, she felt better but she still wasn't 100 percent. Somehow she managed to get through her routines without any missteps. When she was on stage all her worries washed away.

After the show and two curtain calls, Kaia raced to her dressing room and took a quick shower before the other girls could get back there. She quickly dressed because Landon wanted them all to meet in a half hour for a special announcement in his dressing room. She flopped on the couch to rest until then. As with all the shows on this run, the room was full of roses. Blaise had gone over the top as always but it was sweet of him.

Aneka and Blaise came backstage to congratulate her. And as usual, Aneka was in awe of everything.

The troupe was supposed to go out afterward to celebrate since this was the last show but Kaia wasn't up to it so Blaise offered to take her and Aneka out afterward.

Kaia was actually looking forward to it. Blaise said he'd have the car waiting for her behind the building when she was finished with her meeting.

All the dancers crammed themselves into Landon's dressing room. Kaia took the only empty chair in the corner of the room. She was starting to feel sick again. It had to be the flu but if she could get through tonight she'd get to sleep in tomorrow morning because there would be no show or rehearsal.

Landon stood in the middle of the room. "I just wanted to thank everyone for a phenomenal show tonight. We were completely sold out for the entire run and it's all because of your hard work. I want each and every one of you to know that without you, Bodies in Motion would not have been the success that it was." He paused and looked around the room and his eyes focused on hers briefly. For a moment it seemed like she read regret in that gaze but she could have just imagined it.

And why did he refer to the dance company in the past tense? Something about this moment seemed off.

"As you know, it's always been my dream to put on a big production so that my work can be seen all over the world. Many of you may have heard of Edgar Paulson, one of the biggest Broadway producers who has had a number of hits. He's in development to work on a new show and he's looking for choreographers. He's looking for someone fresh with lots of new ideas. He believes that someone is me. And it wasn't an easy decision but I've decided to accept the job. And that means that this will be Bodies in Motions' last show.

Each and every one of you are super talented and I know that other opportunities will come to you. In fact, you're all welcome to audition for the new show I'll be working on. And don't worry, I'll make sure each and every one of you receives a huge bonus in your last checks."

The room went silent. Most of the people looked at each other in shocked disbelief. Someone started to cry and Patty yelled out, "You've got to be fucking kidding me."

Kaia was absolutely numb. It had all been for nothing. She'd sacrificed herself only to for Landon to bail on all of them. Not only had he taken the proverbial knife and shoved it in her back he took it out and stabbed her over and over again. And then he had the nerve to act as if he was doing them all a big fucking favor.

That even Deena looked surprised at Landon's announcement should have given Kaia some comfort but she couldn't help but think of all her friends who were now out of work.

Kaia was so over this. She stood up and walked over to Landon. "You are, the biggest piece of shit there ever was. You've pretended to play the injured party or week and allowed people to call me a whore without telling them the truth. I didn't break up with you to be with Blaise Lundgaard. You wanted me to be with him so you can get the financing for Bodies in Motion. How about you tell your little sycophants that. And now you have the nerve to stand here as if you're not messing with people's livelihoods. Just when I think you can't get any lower you manage to outdo yourself. But I have a feeling that no matter what I say won't register because you're nothing but a narcissist. So here's a little something to remember me by." With all the fury she had within her, Kaia brought her knee up and rammed it into Landon's crotch.

"Oh shit!" he yelled as he dropped to the ground.

Kaia walked out of the room without a backward glance. As she gathered her things she didn't know whether to cry or scream. She certainly didn't feel like celebrating.

As Blaise had promised, the car was waiting for her in the back of the building. There were a few fans in the back waiting for autographs and photos. Kaia went through the motions with them before being ushered to the car by Roger. She slid into the back seat next to Aneka.

"Is everything all right?" Blaise asked.

Kaia didn't know what to say. There was a lump in her throat and any second she felt like she would snap. She simply shook her head.

Aneka lightly touched her shoulder. "What's the matter, Kaia? You look so sad."

Perhaps it was the combined concern from Blaise and Aneka. Maybe it was because she still felt sick and now on top of that she had a pounding headache. Or it could have been the fact that she'd given everything to Bodies in Motion for the last few years only for Landon to betray them all. More than likely it was a combination of everything because she burst into tears and couldn't stop.

I don't understand what's taking them so long. It's been over four hours. Dr. Jefferson said it would only take three hours. Shouldn't someone be out here to give us a progress update?" Kaia asked shifting in her chair impatiently.

Blaise took her hand. "Dr. Jefferson did say that the surgery could be three to four hours. I'm sure if anything goes wrong, they'll let us know."

"How can you be so calm? I'm freaking out here. I mean even Aneka was smiling before the drugs kicked in. You two must have ice water in your veins."

Blaise brought her hand to his mouth and lightly kissed it. "It's because she's a fighter. And I have faith that she'll pull through this. Aneka has been confined to a chair since she was three years old. She was so brave and strong as she went through rehabilitation, even though she was in a lot of pain, she smiled through it. She's been my inspiration for a very long time now, so I refuse to believe that things won't turn out for the best. The surgery will be a success and she will walk again."

"I wish I had your confidence."

"Trust me. Everything will work out as it was meant to be, *kæreste*."

His words put her slightly at ease but she was still a mess. This past week had been an emotional roller coaster for her. She was out of a job, Aneka was having her surgery and she was definitely pregnant.

Kaia had been in denial but the signs were there. Her breasts were tender, her period was late and she was suffering from nausea morning noon and night. Whoever called it morning sickness was full of shit because she was sick all hours of the day. Even certain smells make her gag.

She had discreetly purchased a pregnancy test and it had turned out positive. She didn't know what to do with herself because it would certainly put her dancing on the back burner for a while. Then she thought about her friend Jackie who was a single mother but still managed to dance. It briefly crossed her mind to get rid of it. But she couldn't do it. She had nothing against abortion if that was someone's choice, but Kaia simply didn't have it in her.

She wasn't sure how it happened because she never missed a day of her birth control. She'd been so careful. And what would Blaise think? He was already super possessive of her and with a child in the mix, there was no telling how he'd be. Or he might not want it at all.

Now that Aneka's surgery would be behind them and there was no more dance troupe, then there was no reason to stay. But why did the idea of leaving Blaise and Aneka sadden her? Maybe Blaise had managed to infiltrate her heart these past few months. The hows and whys were still unclear but she'd fallen for Blaise Lundgaard. But what would he say about the baby?

Just then, Dr. Jefferson came out of the O.R.

Blaise and Kaia both stood up.

"How did it go?"

"Surgery went well. Aneka did beautifully. She's in the recovery room right now if you'd like to sit with her Mr. Lundgaard. In the meantime..."

The doctor's words blurred as a wave of nausea she couldn't overcome hit her.

"I'm sorry. Excuse me." She turned around and rushed to the bathroom. She made it to the bathroom stall just in time to throw up everything in her stomach. She didn't eat much earlier because she was too nervous about Aneka's surgery but that didn't matter. By the time she finished, Kaia started to cry.

"What am I going to do?" she whispered to herself.

She sat on the floor of the bathroom for several more moments before getting up to flush. She grabbed a paper towel and wet it to wipe her face. When she felt she looked well enough to return to the lobby she squared her shoulders and walked out of the bathroom only to find Blaise leaning against the wall.

"Is there something you need to tell me?"

There was no point in denying it. He'd find out soon enough anyway. "I don't know how it happened, Blaise. I was so careful." Fresh tears scalded her eyes.

Blaise pulled her into his arms and kissed the top of her head. "These things happen. Don't be upset. I'll take care of you and my child."

He was taking it surprisingly well.

She raised her head. "You're not upset?"

"Of course not. I love you, Kaia. How could I be upset about something that we made together? I know that we got off to a rocky start but I believe that you might love me a little as well?"

She hesitated before answering. "Yes...I do."

He bent down and gave her a light peck on the lips. "I love you, Kaia. And I promise to always cherish you."

She wrapped her arms around his neck and returned his hug.

Finally, when they broke the embrace, he took her by the hand. "Let's go check in on Aneka."

He smiled at her and she had a feeling that everything would be all right.

Epilogue

"You look nervous Kaia. I know for a fact you've flown before." Blaise said from beside his love. She was so beautiful with her hair in a cascade of curls around her face. Her skin practically glowed and it made him hard knowing that she was carrying his child.

"Yes, I have but I've never been on a private jet. This is really nice."

"You deserve the best, my love. But you're not being honest with me. Why are you so nervous?"

"Wouldn't you be if you were moving to another country? I've only been to Denmark once and we only stayed a couple of days. I don't know anyone there except you and Aneka and I don't speak the language. I feel like I'll be a fish out of water."

"You'll make lots of friends and I'll hire a private tutor for you to learn the language. And there are plenty of dance studios in the area. Or I could have a studio built in our home."

"You say that so casually."

"What?"

"Our home."

"It is our home, Kaia. Whatever is mine is yours. And I want you to know that you'll never want for anything. And as a sign of my love for you, I have a present for you."

Kaia shook her head. "Blaise, you've already done so much. Giving the dancers that money to help them out in between jobs was more than generous."

"It was the least I could do after that stunt Campion pulled." He reached into his pocket and pulled out a black velvet box.

Her eyes widened. "This isn't what I think it is."

He opened the box to reveal a ten karat pink heart-shaped diamond. He took it out and slipped it on her left ring finger without waiting for a response.

"Blaise... I don't know what to say," Kaia whispered staring at the ring.

"You're already mine. I'm just making it official."

"Did you ask her yet? Aneka asked from the seat across from them.

Blaise smiled at his sister. "Yes, precious. Kaia and I are getting married.

"I can't wait. Can I be a bridesmaid? I'll be able to walk down the aisle in a pretty dress!" Aneka exclaimed.

The surgery was a success and already Aneka had started to feel some sensation in her legs though there would still be some extensive physical therapy she'd have to undergo.

Blaise turned to a stunned Kaia. "What do you think, *kæreste?* Can Aneka be a bridesmaid?"

"Uh, yes, of course." Kaia looked uncertain but she would get used to the idea once she settled into her new life.

Just then the pilot came on the intercom. "Welcome onboard, Mr. Lundgaard and guests. We have beautiful weather for our flight to Copenhagen."

Blaise turned to Kaia who was still eyeing the ring. There was uncertainty in her gaze. But he would make sure that she was at ease when they arrived home. He would ensure that she was stress-free and had a healthy and safe pregnancy, under his watchful eye of course.

He would go to any lengths for this woman and he had. Some would say he was crazy for replacing her birth control with placebos or calling in a favor with his friend Edgar. But as he'd told Kaia, he wasn't crazy. He was simply thorough.

Very thorough.

Kaia and Blaise's saga continues in...Forever

Obsessed

About the Author

New York Times and USA Today Bestselling Author Eve Vaughn has always enjoyed creating characters and stories from an early age. As a child she was always getting into mischief, so when she lost her television privileges (which was often), writing was her outlet. Her stories have gotten quite a bit spicier since then! When she's not writing or spending time with her family, Eve is reading, baking, traveling or kicking butt in 80's trivia. She loves hearing from her readers. She can be contacted through her website at: www.evevaughn.com.

Books by Eve Vaughn:

Whatever He Wants

Jilted

Dirty

Relentless

Theirs

Runaway

Run

The Reinvention of Chastity

Burned

Made in United States
Orlando, FL
24 October 2025